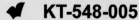
She looked so beautiful it made him ache.

Grace was deliberately not looking at him as she came up the aisle, and was focusing rather intently on the altar straight ahead of her. Still, Bryan couldn't take his eyes off her.

He was struck by the utter rightness of this moment—waiting for her at the front of the church.

What, exactly, did that mean?

Still without looking at him, Grace took her place. The organ music swelled and the members of the audience rose to their feet as the bride entered on the arm of her father. Bryan glanced that way, and then his eyes returned to Grace.

Maybe she felt his attention on her. Or maybe it was only happenstance that she finally looked his way. Their eyes met and held for so long that others must have noticed. But this was no act. It wasn't romantic posturing for the sake of anyone who might be watching them. They looked at each other because they couldn't look away.

And it was then that Bryan knew what had been missing from his life…

Available in June 2003 from Silhouette Special Edition

Woman of Innocence
by Lindsay McKenna
(Morgan's Mercenaries)

The Best Man's Plan
by Gina Wilkins

Big Sky Cowboy
by Jennifer Mikels
(Montana)

Royal Protocol
by Christine Flynn
(Crown and Glory)

The Runaway Bride
by Patricia McLinn

The Marriage Prescription
by Debra Webb
(Colby Agency)

The Best Man's Plan
GINA WILKINS

SILHOUETTE®
SPECIAL EDITION™

*All the characters in this book have no existence outside the imagination
of the author, and have no relation whatsoever to anyone bearing the
same name or names. They are not even distantly inspired by any
individual known or unknown to the author, and all the incidents are
pure invention.*

*First published in Great Britain 2003
Silhouette Books, Eton House, 18-24 Paradise Road,
Richmond, Surrey TW9 1SR*

© Gina Wilkins 2002

ISBN 0 373 24479 7

23-0603

*Printed and bound in Spain
by Litografia Rosés S.A., Barcelona*

GINA WILKINS

is a bestselling and award-winning author who has written more than fifty books for Silhouette. She credits her successful career in romance to her long, happy marriage and her three 'extraordinary' children.

A lifelong resident of central Arkansas, Gina sold her first book to Silhouette in 1987 and has been writing full-time ever since. She has appeared on many bestseller lists. She is a three-time recipient of the Maggie Award for Excellence, sponsored by Georgia Romance Writers, and has won several awards from the reviewers of *Romantic Times Magazine*.

For my longtime, long-distance writing pals, Alison Hart and Patricia McLaughlin. I'm not sure I've ever told you how much your friendship means to me.

Chapter One

"Ms. Pennington! Look this way, please."
Flash.
"Ms. Pennington. Mr. Falcon. Over here."
Flash.
"How about a kiss for the camera?"

Smiling at the devastatingly handsome man who stood at her side with his arm around her, Grace Pennington hissed between her teeth, "Kiss me for these clowns' benefit and you'll end up with bloody lips."

"Darling," he murmured, a glimmer of laughter in his midnight-blue eyes, "you know how it turns me on when you whisper sweet nothings in my ear."

A growl rumbled in her throat, but she managed somehow to keep her forced smile in place. *For Chloe,* she reminded herself. This was all for Chloe.

Another bright flash nearly blinded her and then, to her immense relief, she and Bryan reached the limo where a driver waited beside an open door. The paparazzi had already turned their frenetic attentions to the next prominent couple who had just emerged from the theater.

"Good," Bryan murmured with a glance over his shoulder, "they've spotted the Gates. Now Bill can deal with them for a while."

Gathering her long skirt in both hands, Grace ducked into the limo. She almost whimpered in gratitude when the driver closed the door, and she and Bryan were alone in the welcome silence of the vehicle's luxurious interior. Her fake smile immediately faded, letting her aching cheeks rest.

"I hated that pretentious event. And I think I hate you," she added, glowering at her escort.

He laughed, showing a flash of white teeth. "You've made that clear since the day we met. But you do love your sister."

She sighed, unable to argue with that. Only her love for her twin could have brought her to this glittering charity event, or involved her in the ridiculous charade she and Bryan Falcon had been orchestrating for the past two weeks.

She pushed a hand through her spray-stiffened hair, dislodging a crystal-encrusted clip that had been holding a sweep of brown hair from her face. The heavy lock fell onto her cheek, curving below her chin in a semblance of her usual casual bob. Tugging at the low top of her strapless black gown, she nudged off the tortuous high heels she had suffered all evening. The heavy diamond earrings that had been pinching her earlobes were the next to go; she stuffed them into her evening bag and tossed it aside.

Still immaculate in his crisp tuxedo, his black hair

neatly swept back from a face that had graced several photo spreads of the country's most eligible bachelors, Bryan watched her shed the sophisticated façade she had grudgingly donned several hours earlier. "Need help unzipping?"

Since she wore nothing beneath the gown but a few scraps of lace, she merely glared at him in response. She thought longingly of jeans, T-shirts and well-worn sneakers—none of which she had on hand at the moment, unfortunately.

"Would you like some champagne?" he asked, motioning toward the built-in bar. "Wine?"

"Got a diet cola in there?"

"I'll check."

A minute later she had a cold can in her hand, having refused a glass. Popping the top, she poured caffeine-laced, artificially sweetened liquid down her throat. Through the glass partition ahead of her, she could see the back of the driver's head as he navigated the crowded streets away from the theater.

After watching her unwind for a moment, Bryan asked, "Did you really hate the opera that much? The event was for a good cause."

"The fund-raiser was certainly worthwhile. Of course, most of the overdressed, anorexic guests preening for the paparazzi and patting themselves on their scrawny backs could have donated more than the price of a ticket if they'd just tossed in one of the glittering baubles decorating their malnourished bodies—and that was just the men."

Bryan made a funny sound in the back of his throat, but his expression didn't change. "And the program, itself?"

"Opera isn't really my type of music. I'm sure the

performers were very good at what they do, but I can't say I enjoyed it. Since I didn't understand the words, I found the story hard to follow—and what I did understand seemed awfully depressing. It just got sadder and sadder and then everyone died.''

''That pretty much sums up the plot,'' he murmured, though she suspected he had enjoyed the performance more than she had.

She sighed. ''Okay, I'm being ungracious. It's just that I hate this whole charade. The way everyone watches us and speculates about us. The catty tittering about Chloe and Donovan. The security. I *really* hate the security. Couldn't we—?''

His smiling eyes hardened. ''We've discussed this. The security is not negotiable. I'm not willing to risk your safety.''

''You don't really think someone else will decide to try a kidnapping scheme, do you? Especially since it failed so badly last time, with all three kidnappers now in custody and the mastermind behind the plan still on the run after jumping his bail.''

''I'm relatively confident that Childers has left the country. I've received reports that he was spotted in Mexico and probably has moved to South America. But until I know for sure where that bastard is hiding, I won't be entirely satisfied—and neither will Donovan. And I'm not willing to bet your safety that someone else won't get the stupid idea of tapping into my money by grabbing someone I care about. So long as we're together—even if it's only for the benefit of the gossip columnists—you'll tolerate the security.''

She reminded herself that Bryan was a man accustomed to being in command. A man who wielded a great deal of power in his business and an almost equal amount of influence socially. He was used to giving orders and having them followed without question, so she shouldn't get so irritated every time he took that officious tone with her.

It still hacked her off.

"I'll tolerate the security until after Chloe's wedding," she conceded, her voice frosty. "But I don't have to like it."

"No." His smile had returned now. "You don't have to like it. Or me, for that matter—as long as we keep those feelings just between us."

The limo hit a bump in the road, causing Grace to slide on the leather seat. Bryan reached out quickly to steady her, his hand warm on her bare arm. The strength she sensed in him each time he touched her always surprised her. It belied his appearance of lazy elegance—a façade she suspected he cultivated deliberately so his opponents would underestimate him.

It wasn't a mistake most people made more than once.

The drive to the Manhattan hotel where they would be spending the night didn't take long. Grace sighed as the limo glided to a stop at the door. Somehow she was going to have to wedge her feet into those gosh-awful heels again. She groped with her right foot, then scowled when her abused toes throbbed in protest.

"Hell with it," she muttered, and reached down to scoop up the shoes by their delicate ankle straps. "I'll carry them."

Bryan's smile deepened just perceptibly at the corners, irritating her even more. Someday she was going to wipe that smirk right off his handsome face. She was not here to amuse him, damn it.

The driver opened the door and extended a hand to

her. Ignoring it, she climbed out, clutching her shoes in one hand and the top of her dress with the other. The lock of hair that had escaped the clip tumbled into her face. She blew it back.

She glanced at her perfectly pressed companion, who had moved to her side. Even holding the delicate evening bag she had forgotten, he looked impeccably masculine—and amused again.

"*Now* what are you grinning about?"

There was a wicked gleam in his eyes when he gave her a leisurely survey. "You look as though we had quite an...interesting ride," he murmured.

Her cheeks flamed as she pictured herself standing there barefoot, her hair and dress in suspicious disarray. The blush probably only reinforced the image of a woman who'd just played tease-and-tickle in the back of a limo. Accidentally catching the eye of a rotund man across the lobby, she saw him raise an eyebrow—apparently in recognition of her escort—and then smile in a way that confirmed her suspicion of the impression her mussed appearance conveyed. "Damn it."

Even though it was exactly the image they were trying to portray, it still galled her to think that everyone around them was engaged in salacious speculation about what had gone on between her and Bryan in the limo—and what would go on between them in the luxury penthouse suite he'd booked for the night. She might have stalked brusquely toward the elevators right then, sending off-putting glares toward anyone who dared catch her eye, had Bryan not slipped an arm around her waist and pulled her firmly to his side.

"We don't want to give the appearance that we've

had a spat,'' he reminded her, his mouth very close to her ear. Anyone watching them would probably have imagined that he was murmuring suggestions of what he would like to do to her when he got her upstairs. "Play your part," he added.

She'd agreed to do this, and she wasn't going to have anyone—especially Bryan—say she hadn't been good at it. Turning her head just enough so that her lips brushed his jaw as she spoke, she murmured, "What do you suppose they would think if I ram my elbow into your abdomen right now?''

He chuckled, the sound just a bit husky. "Maybe that I'm into the dominatrix scene?''

"Not something I've been interested in, myself." She nuzzled lightly just beneath his ear. "But with you, I just might enjoy wielding the whip.''

He took her completely off guard by planting a firm kiss directly on her mouth. "I'll keep that in mind," he said when he finally released her.

He caught her fist an inch from his stomach and, lifting it to his lips, drew her into an empty elevator. He made his moves so swiftly that she was sure no one realized he'd just missed having the breath knocked out of him. But they'd certainly put on a show, anyway, she thought with a stifled sigh.

The moment the elevator doors closed completely, she broke away from Bryan and moved across the small car. Since she couldn't physically injure him— the darned male was just too fast for her—she contented herself with stabbing him with angry glares.

"Must you look at me that way?'' he inquired. "I feel my eyebrows starting to singe.''

"That kiss was completely unnecessary.''

"I thought it added a nice touch.'' He actually

looked smug as he brushed a nonexistent smudge from his jacket. "I imagine we gave the gossips enough fodder to chew on for a few days."

"Good. Can we go home now?"

"You wound me with your eagerness to be rid of my company."

She gave a low growl of exasperation. "And would you *please* stop talking like a character in a Regency romance novel?"

He laughed and motioned toward the opening elevator doors. "Sorry. I guess I got carried away with the role of devoted suitor."

"You think?" Holding her chin high—and her shoes tightly—she swept ahead of him out of the elevator. The overall effect was probably diminished somewhat when she stumbled over her long skirt, but she righted herself almost immediately, ignoring the steadying hand Bryan held out to her.

Bryan had booked a two-bedroom suite. Grace would have insisted on that, of course, but he had done so without asking. She didn't particularly care what the gossips made of their arrangements, and neither did Bryan, apparently. She turned immediately toward the bedroom she had claimed earlier. "I'll see you in the morning."

"No good-night kiss?"

She threw a shoe at him.

Catching the strappy sandal in one hand, he grinned. "Sleep well, Grace."

Sleep well? Fat chance.

More as a defiant gesture than a belief that the precaution was necessary, she locked her bedroom door after closing it in Bryan's face.

* * *

Only after changing into an oversized T-shirt and plaid pajama pants, her face scrubbed clean and every trace of hairspray brushed from her hair, did Grace feel more like herself. Now if only she were home…

Glancing at the clock on the nightstand, she noted that it was past midnight. Yet it was an hour earlier back home. Maybe Chloe would still be awake. She was suddenly almost overcome with the urge to hear her sister's voice—if for no other reason than to remind herself why she was here.

Sounding wide-awake, Chloe answered on the second ring. "Hello?"

"Hi, it's Grace. I hope I didn't wake you."

"No, I've been going over some paperwork from the store. Donovan's helping me."

Grace imagined that Donovan's "help" had only made the task take twice as long, but she kept that opinion to herself. "We've just gotten back from that charity opera thing."

"How was it?"

Dozens of complaints hovered on her tongue, but she settled for just one. "People kept staring at us."

"Get used to it. Whenever you're with Bryan Falcon, people will stare. Even when you're in a place where no one recognizes him—rare as those places are—there's something about him that somehow commands attention."

Grace was well aware of that, of course. She'd often wondered if people stared at Bryan because of his extraordinary good looks, or that air of quiet power that surrounded him like a royal mantle. Whatever the reason, it was still unnerving.

"How was the evening other than that? Did you

see lots of celebrities in beautiful dresses? Did you enjoy the program?''

Because the whole point of this charade was to make Chloe happy, Grace had vowed not to complain to her sister. She would save all her gripes for Bryan, who deserved them because this whole crazy scheme had been his idea—and just because he was Bryan. ''It was fine. And yes, I saw tons of celebrities. I'm sure you would have enjoyed the evening—though I'm not so certain Donovan would have.''

''Probably not. Though he would have gone if he thought I really wanted to be there.''

Grace had no doubt of that. Donovan Chance spoiled her sister shamelessly. A battered warrior who didn't express his feelings easily, Donovan seemed determined to make a success of this relationship— the first that had truly mattered to him, apparently. Donovan was almost fanatically loyal to those he cared most about—a very short list topped by Chloe and Bryan, his employer and best friend since high school.

Since Chloe's happiness was paramount to her, too, Grace fully approved of her sister's choice of a mate. This time, at least. She hadn't felt at all the same way when Chloe had been considering marriage to Bryan Falcon.

The sisters talked a few more minutes and then Grace brought the call to an end. Wandering to a window to gaze out at the colorfully lit city so far and so different from her hometown, she thought about the quiet contentment that was always present in Chloe's voice these days. Knowing that she was contributing to that happiness, if only in a minor way, gave her mixed feelings. She was glad to be able to help, but now she felt even more trapped in this ridiculous scam.

"Trapped" was a feeling she had grown to know all too well during the past couple of years.

So maybe it hadn't been the brightest idea he'd ever had. Convincing Grace to pretend to be romantically involved with him had been difficult enough—following through with the improbable scheme was proving to be even more complicated. It didn't help, of course, that Grace couldn't stand him.

Sprawled on his hotel-room bed with the TV remote in one hand and a glass of orange juice in the other, Bryan mentally replayed the number of close calls he had averted that evening—most notably, the moment when he'd narrowly avoided being drilled in the stomach by her fist. She'd packed quite a punch, too. If he hadn't managed to catch her hand and pull it away, she'd have doubled him over. And wouldn't *that* have caught some attention in tomorrow's gossip columns?

He probably shouldn't have given in to that impulse to kiss her. But he hadn't tried very hard to resist. Kissing Grace Pennington was something he'd been tempted to do for several weeks now, to his own surprise and her obvious dismay.

After knowing her for nearly six months, he still wasn't quite sure what it was about him that aroused so much antagonism in her. Her twin had liked him from the moment of their chance meeting last winter when he'd wandered into Mirror Images, the decorating shop Chloe and Grace owned and operated in Little Rock's River Market district. He and Chloe had struck up a conversation that had continued over coffee and then into several dinner dates.

Less than a month into their friendship, he'd brought up the subject of marriage.

He hadn't even pretended to be in love with Chloe. He had liked her very much, admired and respected her a great deal. He'd found her attractive, but he knew the difference between simple affection and the passionate love hyped in literature and song. But after carefully observing and studying the few successful marriages among his many acquaintances, he had come to the conclusion that the most enduring basis for a lifelong partnership was genuine friendship.

He'd tried the more popular methods of courtship, letting himself be led by his heart—and other, more primitive body parts. He'd ended up involved in several volatile relationships with beautiful, talented, famous—and usually completely self-centered—actresses and models. He'd thought women already accustomed to fame and fortune would have been more likely to value him for himself rather than what he could give them. He'd been wrong.

Those high-profile disasters had led to embarrassment, disillusion, and the unwelcome attentions of the tabloid writers, who had been as intrigued by his dating adventures as they were fascinated by his innate flair for making fortunes.

''I've been going about this courtship thing the wrong way,'' he had concluded to Donovan during the last Thanksgiving holidays. ''I'd never invest in a business venture on impulse or emotion. I choose my investments based on rational and carefully determined criteria, all focused on the probability of success. That's the way I need to select a wife. Someone I like and respect and who feels the same way about me. Someone with similar values and interests, with compatible goals and dreams. Someone who wants a family as much as I do, and who'll put the welfare of the family ahead of everything else—as I plan to do.''

''What about love?'' Donovan had asked doubtfully. ''Passion? All those other things the romantics say should be part of getting married? Not that I ever intend to try it myself, but...''

That, of course, had been before Donovan met Chloe—back when he'd been convinced that he would remain a bachelor for the rest of his life. Bryan was the one who, facing his thirty-ninth birthday, had decided he wanted to get married. Who had wanted a family. A home. And when he'd met Chloe, he believed he'd found a perfect potential mate.

Chloe met nearly every qualification on his carefully thought-out list—and she had admitted that she, too, had been disappointed with traditional dating rituals. Though nearly ten years younger than Bryan, she had begun to wonder if she would ever have the children she'd always wanted.

It had seemed like a match made in marriage-of-convenience heaven. According to Bryan's calculations, an alliance between them had better than eighty percent odds of success—much better probability than the typical marriage, which stood only a fifty-fifty chance of lasting.

What he couldn't have predicted was that Chloe would tumble head-over-heels in love with his second in command—and vice versa—making all Bryan's logical, practical planning moot.

A sudden crash from the other room made him jump to his feet, muscles tensed, senses on full alert. Crossing the room in three long strides, he threw open the bedroom door, poised for battle if necessary.

Chapter Two

Grace was crouched on the floor beside the sitting room wet bar, plucking pieces of glass from the thick cream-colored carpet, when Bryan burst through his bedroom door. Had she not seen this aspect of him before, she might have been surprised that her rather lazily graceful, studiedly charming companion of earlier had been transformed into this tightly wound, almost dangerous-looking man. Bryan had looked just this way when Chloe and Donovan were kidnapped, scaring the con artist behind the plot so badly that he'd literally feared for his life.

"I dropped a glass," she said quickly, realizing what had precipitated his tumultuous entrance. "I hope I didn't wake you."

"I wasn't asleep." Moving more slowly now, he crossed the room, his bare feet making no sound on the plush carpeting. "Are you okay? Did you cut yourself?"

"I'm fine." She rose and dropped the shards into a plastic-lined metal wastebasket. They landed with a tinkling, almost cheerfully musical sound. Though her fuzzy blue slippers protected her own feet, she felt obligated to warn him, "I think I found all the pieces, but be careful walking around over here with bare feet."

He'd changed from his tuxedo into a white V-necked T-shirt and a pair of gray sweatpants. His formerly neatly brushed hair was now tousled around his face. And he looked just as gorgeous as he had in the tailored tuxedo earlier.

She had long since grown accustomed to the unwelcome flutter she felt every time she saw him. No matter how he was dressed, Bryan Falcon was undeniably the best-looking man Grace had ever met. Usually she could ignore the sensations, but it was a bit harder in the late-night intimacy of this private suite, with both of them dressed in their ultracasual lounging clothes.

He leaned against one end of the bar. "Having a little trouble unwinding?"

She shrugged and took another glass from the cabinet beside the bar. "I'm just thirsty."

"There's a pitcher of fresh-squeezed orange juice in the fridge. I like to have a glass before bedtime."

"Another one of your special requests?" she asked as she opened the door to the small refrigerator built discreetly into the custom woodwork.

"Yes."

"It must be nice to have everything you want at your fingertips."

"It is," he agreed equably. Apparently he wasn't going to let her push any of his buttons tonight.

He nodded when she motioned with the pitcher, silently asking him if he wanted a glass. She filled an extra one and handed it to him.

He carried the glass to the sofa and sat on one end. After hesitating a moment, she perched on a chair arranged in conversation-group fashion nearby. She thought their casual clothing looked incongruous against the very formal gold-and-cream upholstery, but Bryan was obviously accustomed to making himself comfortable in such rooms. He lounged back against the cushions and crossed his bare feet on the low mahogany table in front of him.

"Are we still on for our high-profile lunch tomorrow?" he asked. "Or would you rather bail out and go home early?"

She wondered if he suspected how tempted she was to accept that escape, but she shook her head. "You said being seen around town together would strengthen the impression that we're a couple. That's what we came here to do."

"You think you can get through an entire meal without dumping a plate of food in my lap?"

"You think *you* can get through an entire meal without making me mad enough to dump a plate of food in your lap?" she countered.

He grinned. "I can try."

Her lips tilted into an answered smile. "Then so will I."

It was so rare for them to smile at each other that the moment caught her off guard. When she realized that he was suddenly staring at her mouth, her smile faded.

Lifting his gaze to her eyes, he asked, "What is it about me, exactly, that annoys you so much? Just so I don't end up with food in my lap tomorrow."

She looked down into her orange juice. "I promise I won't throw food in your lap tomorrow. I know how important it is for us to divert the gossips' attention away from Chloe and Donovan so they can plan their wedding in peace."

"Actually, throwing food at me would be a very effective way of diverting attention to us."

She wrinkled her nose. "Not the right type of attention, perhaps."

He shrugged, keeping his gaze on her face. "I'm serious, Grace. What is it about me that you dislike so much? I know you didn't approve of me as a potential suitor for your sister, but that's over. So…is it something I said? Something I did? You don't like the way I walk? Talk? Smell?"

She couldn't help smiling again. "You smell quite nice, actually. Very expensive."

His left eyebrow rose in an expression that some might call sardonic. "Old Spice. My housekeeper picks it up for me at Wal-Mart when she buys groceries and cleaning supplies. It was the scent my grandfather wore, and I've always been rather fond of it."

She blinked. "Oh."

"That surprises you."

"I'm not surprised that you have a housekeeper. Probably one for every house you own."

"So it's my money that bothers you."

She squirmed uncomfortably on the chair. "Let's

just say I'm not accustomed to the kind of wealth and power you command.''

"Would you like me better if I gave it all away?"

Frowning, she shook her head. "No. I mean—"

"So it isn't entirely the money. It's me you don't like."

She sighed gustily. "I never said I don't like you."

"Actually I believe you said you hated me."

She gave him a reproachful look. "You know I didn't mean that. I was just blowing off steam after that awkward evening."

"So you *do* like me?"

Making a faint sound of frustration, she set her half-empty glass on the coffee table with a thump. "I barely know you, Bryan. You swept into my sister's life, and almost convinced her to enter into a very businesslike marriage with you. I didn't approve of that scheme because I know Chloe deserves better than that—she deserves the happiness she's found with Donovan."

"She met Donovan because of me," he reminded her.

"She was also kidnapped and put through four days of hell because of you," she retorted, making him wince. "And now the gossip columnists are titillated by the possibility that Chloe jilted you, one of the richest, most influential men in the country—a man who made the news a year or so ago for breaking up with one of the most beautiful and famous starlets in the world. And now Chloe's marrying your best friend and business associate, instead. That vicious prattle has mortified Donovan—who's so obsessively loyal to you that he almost broke Chloe's heart rather than risk betraying you with her. And knowing that

Donovan is upset bothers Chloe so badly that it was affecting her joy in planning her wedding."

"I'm aware that her association with me has caused problems for Chloe," he acknowledged stiffly. "That's why I wanted to take some of the pressure off her by leading the gossips away. Since she and I only dated a short time before the press found out about her—so briefly and discreetly that they were never quite sure which Pennington twin I was court-ing—this seemed like the ideal scheme. Now that Chloe's engaged to Donovan and you and I are acting like an established couple, the gossips are beginning to wonder if they had it wrong at the start. If Chloe and Donovan met and fell in love because you and I were already seeing each other, rather than the other way around."

"I hope that's what they believe, anyway," Grace muttered, thinking that all this trouble would be wasted if they hadn't fooled anyone.

"Several are already beginning to speculate in print that the natural confusion that results when two best friends date identical twins is what led to Chloe and Donovan being kidnapped. They believe Wallace Childers had them snatched because he thought I would pay any amount of money to ensure the safety of my best friend and my fiancée."

"Which was pretty much what he *was* thinking. He underestimated you, of course, as well as Donovan. He didn't realize that Donovan would escape so quickly with Chloe, or that you had so many re-sources at your fingertips to track down the identity of the kidnappers."

"I learned a long time ago that having a lot of money means being targeted occasionally by people who want to help themselves to some of it. That's why I've made security such a priority in my organization.''

"I'm well aware of that,'' she muttered, thinking of the discreet, but ever-present bodyguards who had shadowed her so frequently during the past few weeks.

"Cheer up. The wedding's only a month away. After that, we can cut back on the number of public appearances, and eventually stop them altogether. We'll simply imply that we've drifted apart—though we will, of course, decide to remain friends, since we'll be seeing each other often through Donovan and Chloe.''

"Once we've ended this ridiculous playacting, there's no reason at all we shouldn't be friendly with each other.''

"No reason at all,'' he parroted gravely.

She'd amused him again. She supposed she should be used to it by now.

She pushed herself off the chair. "It's getting late. We'd better get some sleep.''

"I'm sure you're right.'' Following her lead, he removed his feet from the table and stood. He carried his empty glass to the wet bar, stopping to take hers on the way. "I'll just put these in the sink....''

She had just reached her bedroom doorway when Bryan made an odd sound behind her. She glanced over her shoulder, then grimaced when she saw his expression. She knew immediately what must have happened. "You've stepped on a piece of glass, haven't you?''

He lifted his right foot, leaving a smear of bright red on the cream-colored carpet. "I'm afraid so.''

* * *

Bryan half expected Grace to chew him out for being careless enough to step on a piece of glass. Instead she hurried toward him, a frown of concern on her face. "Let me see."

"It's no big deal. Just a small…"

She already had her hands on him, pushing him toward one of the two tall wooden stools that flanked the bar. "Let me see."

A bit surprised by her vehemence, he sat and allowed her to bend over his foot. He couldn't help inhaling rather sharply when she gingerly touched the sharp wedge of glass sticking out of the wound.

Her frown deepening, she pulled her hand back. "I have a small first-aid kit in my room. Sit still and I'll get it."

"I'm sure I can—"

Pointing a finger in his face, she said, "Do not move."

He settled more comfortably on the stool. "Yes, ma'am."

She wasn't gone long. Returning with a small plastic box, she opened it and laid it on the bar. He could see that it held a thermometer, single dose packs of pain reliever, fever reducer and antibacterial cream, alcohol pads, tweezers, a small pair of scissors and adhesive bandages in assorted sizes. "You seem to be well equipped for emergencies."

She had already taken his foot in her hands again. "I like to be prepared. This will probably sting when I remove the glass."

"I can take it." Braced for her touch this time, he didn't even flinch when she eased the glass from his foot. He was somewhat surprised by the gentleness of her touch. Based on his past experiences with her, he might have expected her to be a bit rougher with him. Even when she cleaned the bleeding wound with an alcohol pad, she took such care that he hardly noticed the unavoidable burning. "You're quite good at this."

Reaching for the medicated cream and bandages, she sounded distracted when she answered. "I have some experience. My former fiancé was into rodeo. Fancied himself a cowboy. I was always patching him up after…"

She stopped in midsentence, as if she'd caught herself saying something inappropriate. When she spoke again, it was a brusque, "There. That should keep you from bleeding all over this pretty rug. The cut wasn't very deep. I don't think it will give you any problems."

He waited until she had turned to close the first-aid kit before asking very casually, "Fiancé?"

"Ex-fiancé." She closed the plastic box with a snap. "And, no, I don't want to talk about him."

"Fine."

"Fine. Can you walk on that foot?"

He stood, paying little attention to the twinge of discomfort. His concentration was focused, instead, on Grace's flustered expression. "No problem. You've patched me up quite nicely."

"Yes, well, don't expect me to make a habit of it. I just felt bad because I was the one who broke the glass."

He nodded, amused by her gruffly self-conscious tone. Grace was cute when she was embarrassed, though he knew better than to say so aloud. A remark like that could earn him a few more injuries—inten-

tional on her part next time. But it seemed he liked
to live dangerously. "I don't suppose you'd like to
kiss and make it better?"

She lifted an eyebrow and gave him a cool once-
over. "Did you just suggest that I kiss your foot?"

He chuckled. "Darling, you can kiss any part of
me you'd like."

Keeping her chin high, she seemed to make an effort to reply nonchalantly. "Save it for the tabloids,
Falcon."

He was grinning again when she closed her bedroom door behind her with suspicious speed.

Cute, he thought. Grace Pennington was definitely
cute. Even if she was very likely to drop-kick him if
he told her so.

"High profile" was definitely the term to describe
the lunch Bryan treated Grace to just after noon on
Saturday. He'd selected a trendy restaurant known for
hosting celebrities who wanted to be seen while pretending to be incognito. The owner/chef hosted his
own television program and was almost as famous as
the majority of his patrons. The most successful gossip columnists had their own regular tables where
they could eavesdrop in undisturbed silence.

Bryan played to his audience shamelessly, treating
Grace to such solicitous attention that she wouldn't
have been surprised if he'd started spouting sonnets.
He kept an arm around her as he escorted her to their
cozy little table, sat very close to her, rarely looked
away from her. She tried to play her part as convinc-
ingly, looking back at him with what she hoped would
be perceived as an adoring gaze, but mostly she just
felt self-conscious and silly.

"You're doing fine," Bryan murmured at one point during the meal, as if sensing her doubts. He covered her hand on the table with his own, giving a bracing squeeze. "I doubt that anyone here knows how much you would love to pour your ice water over my head."

She couldn't help smiling. "I must be a better actor than I thought."

Bryan was even better. Toying with her fingers with the ease of someone intimately familiar with her body, he murmured, "Darling, I imagine you're very good at anything you put your mind to."

She hated herself for blushing at the unmistakable innuendo in his tone—and for the shivery little sensations that seemed to be running from her palm, where his thumb was making slow, lazy circles, all the way to the pit of her stomach.

He was entirely too good at this. If she wasn't careful, she could start believing that he found her very attractive.

She tugged her hand from his, annoyed to realize that it wasn't quite steady when she reached for her water glass. "I think it would be better if—"

"Mr. Falcon. What a nice surprise to run in to you today."

The man who had stopped by their table, interrupting Grace's words, was tall, slender and very fashionably dressed. His bleached, moussed and sprayed hair swept back from a face tanned in a salon, tucked in a plastic surgeon's office, and accented with vivid-blue contact lenses and pearly white dental caps. It took Grace only a moment to put a name to that striking face; she had seen him a few times on the entertainment channel, where he regularly dished celebrity tidbits and dissed their choice of clothing.

Bryan flashed one of his famous smiles, and Grace couldn't help noticing that he needed no artificial enhancements to make him gorgeous. Nature had taken care of that quite adequately, from his silky black hair to those naturally blue eyes in a face that had made many a red-blooded woman go weak in the knees. Grace's own knees showed a distressing tendency to fail around him—and she didn't even like him very much. Or so she regularly reminded herself.

After exchanging a few meaningless pleasantries with the other man, Bryan turned to Grace. "I don't believe you two have met. Grace Pennington, this is Terence Bishop."

"Yes, of course. I've seen you on television," she said, extending a hand.

His fingers were cold, his grip a bit weak—or maybe that was only in comparison to Bryan's warm, firm touch. He seemed pleased that she had recognized him. "It's delightful to meet you, Ms. Pennington. Are you enjoying your visit to our city?"

"Yes, very much, thank you."

She could see him cataloging her simple hairstyle and the conservative cut of her emerald-green blouse and oatmeal linen slacks. He'd also noted the rhythm of her Southern accent. "You're from Arkansas, aren't you?" he asked as if he found it hard to believe that anyone would actually choose to live in such a place.

"Little Rock," she confirmed with a determinedly pleasant nod. "Have you been there?"

"Oh, goodness no." He appeared to be amused by the very idea. "I seem to always be flying from one coast to the other, with very few stops in between."

"Then you've missed a great many fascinating places," Bryan inserted smoothly. "I grew up in Little Rock, you know, and I still maintain a home there, though I don't get to spend as much time there as I would like now."

Bishop's gaze turned speculative as he looked from Bryan to Grace. "I understand you've been spending quite a lot of time there lately."

Bryan sent Grace a warm smile. "As much as I can manage."

"You led the press on quite a chase, you know." Bishop shook a finger in a gesture of indulgent reprimand. "That was very tricky of you to keep everyone guessing which lovely twin you were actually dating."

Bryan shrugged. "My personal life is my business, of course. Still, I noticed that most got it wrong. You were one of the ones who reported that I was all but engaged to Grace's sister, weren't you, Terence?"

A faint touch of red stained the other man's throat, but he managed a credible chuckle. "I'm afraid so. And you did nothing to set us straight. You practically confirmed that you were seeing Zoe—"

"Chloe," Grace corrected in a mutter.

"Ah, yes, of course. But you must admit it appeared as though your old friend swept in and wooed your fiancée away from you. It's quite a coincidence that you and Mr. Chance fell for sisters, don't you think?"

Bryan's grin deepened. "The dreaded love triangle—another bit of gossip fabricated through sloppy reporting. At least you've managed to avoid that one—haven't you, Terence?"

"Certainly. I finally remembered how much you enjoy toying with the media. That wicked sense of humor just might lead you into trouble someday, Mr. Falcon.''

''I'll keep your warning in mind. Yet, while the media was busy trying to figure out the players, Grace and I had a chance to get to know each other in relative private, didn't we, darling?''

She only smiled when he took her hand again.

''So—'' Looking searchingly from Bryan to Grace again, Bishop asked bluntly, ''Can we expect another wedding announcement in the family soon?''

''One wedding at a time is plenty for my family, Mr. Bishop,'' Grace replied. ''Bryan and I are quite happy as we are for now. Isn't that right, *darling?*''

He lifted her hand to his lips. ''Deliriously.''

Their gazes met and held over her hand. Grace found herself momentarily unable to look away, captured by the gleam in his eyes and the brush of his mouth against her palm. Her fingers curled inward almost instinctively, as if to prevent the kiss from escaping.

Bishop cleared his throat. ''Well. I'll leave you lovebirds to finish your meal. Perhaps we'll see each other again soon.''

Bryan looked away, breaking that disconcerting moment of connection with Grace. ''I'm sure we will.''

''And you will let me know if there are any announcements in the future, won't you?''

''You'll be the first to know,'' Bryan replied with such cheerful insincerity that Bishop was almost sulking when he strolled away.

Bryan turned back to Grace. ''I think that went well, don't you?''

His sudden transformation from devoted suitor to smug co-conspirator made Grace blink. Pulling herself together quickly, she snarled, "You licked my hand, you degenerate."

He laughed softly. "And you taste delectable—as I suspected you would."

She scooted nearer to him, gazing up at him through her lashes and keeping her voice a low, husky croon. "Bryan?"

His gaze fell to her moistened lips. "Mmm?"

Some evil impulse made her lean even closer, well aware that the neckline of her blouse gaped when she did so. In typical male fashion, his gaze dropped lower. "When this is all over—"

"Yes?" he prodded without raising his eyes.

She straightened away from him. "I'm going to have you killed."

He laughed and reached for his water glass. "It's always nice to have something to look forward to."

Chloe and Donovan were waiting at the airport when Grace and Bryan arrived in Little Rock early that evening. Chloe rushed forward to greet them, Donovan following a bit more slowly at her heels.

It still startled Grace at times to see the short, fashionably choppy hairstyle her twin had sported for the past few months. They'd always worn similar styles in the past—and Grace had traditionally been the one to break rank and try something new. They'd stopped dressing alike in elementary school, and had maintained separate apartments for years, but their lives had still been tightly intertwined, both personally and professionally. Grace was aware that many things would be changing between them once Chloe and Donovan married and formed their own family.

Chloe hugged her, then stepped back to look at her as though it had been longer than a couple of days since they'd seen each other. "Did you have a good time in New York?"

"It was very nice," Grace answered without a blink.

Glancing quickly around them, Chloe lowered her voice to a conspiratorial whisper. "Do you think you accomplished your goal? Keeping the gossips confused about us, I mean."

Grace smiled with a patience she reserved only for Chloe. "I know what our goal was. And, yes, I think we made some progress on that front."

Bryan and Donovan had greeted each other with slaps on the shoulders—a ritual Grace had always considered the male version of a hug. Bryan then turned to Chloe, taking her hand in both of his and bending to brush a kiss across her cheek, murmuring a complimentary greeting as he did so.

Tucking a lock of hair behind her ear, Grace watched the interplay between Bryan and her sister, trying to read his expression. Only a few short months ago he had asked Chloe to marry him. Though he'd seemed to accept Chloe's relationship with Donovan graciously enough, Grace couldn't help wondering how he really felt about Chloe now. Surely he'd had some sort of strong feelings for her if he'd actually considered spending the rest of his life with her, raising children with her. Frankly Grace couldn't imagine anyone not loving Chloe.

But Bryan had managed to move on from several previous relationships without ever looking back—at least according to those gossip columnists who'd been making their lives so stressful lately.

They all pretended not to notice the attention they received from others in the airport terminal, though all four were aware they'd been recognized by at least a few. When Bryan draped an arm casually around Grace's shoulders, drawing her closer to him as they headed for the exit behind Chloe and Donovan, she knew he was making sure they were seen as a couple. She saw Chloe slant them a sideways glance, but she didn't return the look. If she was going to bluff her way through this, she couldn't meet Chloe's eyes.

They went out to dinner, choosing a restaurant that was popular enough to keep them in the public eye, yet quiet enough to allow them to talk comfortably. Though they chatted about Grace and Bryan's trip to New York, they were careful not to even obliquely refer to the purpose for that excursion. They were always aware of the possibility of being overheard.

Grace wondered how Bryan could stand living such a fishbowl existence. The average wealthy businessman could live in relative privacy, but Bryan, with his extraordinary looks and influential, highly visible circle of friends and associates, was hardly average. Something about him had drawn the interest of the media from the time he'd broken away from his prominent family's long-successful business holdings to strike out on his own, finding success at a very early age, even in the era of twenty-something multimillionaires. His predilection for beautiful and famous women had placed him solidly in the gossip columns, even though he'd once told Chloe that he'd long since moved beyond that fascination.

Still, a man with his looks, his money and his access to the most exclusive social circles was bound to stir the imaginations of a celebrity-obsessed society, and Bryan hadn't been able to take himself out of the public eye once he'd moved into it. Rather than running from the attention and becoming a privacy-obsessed hermit, he had learned, instead, to manipulate it—as he was doing now with Grace. There were still drawbacks to the fame, of course—the constant awareness of security among the worst, in her opinion, but he seemed to be comfortable enough with his life as far as Grace could determine.

She wondered if he'd given up on finding a suitable mate to share that life with, or if he was only waiting until after Chloe and Donovan's wedding to resume his carefully calculated search.

Not that she was particularly interested in Bryan Falcon's future private life, she assured herself, even as he asked for the benefit of a hovering waiter, "Would you like dessert, darling? The strawberry cheesecake is excellent here."

The one thing she looked forward to when this farce was over was shoving his "darlings" right back in his pretty face. Grace made sure no hint of that rather ferocious fantasy was evident when she smiled and murmured sweetly, "No, I'm fine, thank you."

She could tell from the gleam in his eyes that he'd guessed at least the essence of her thoughts. They'd been spending entirely too much time together if they were starting to read each other's thoughts, she promptly decided.

Chloe was watching them again, and for some reason that made Grace uncomfortable. Though they'd never had that eerie psychic bond some identical twins claimed, there were times Grace had to make a real effort to keep Chloe from reading her too closely. There were aspects of Grace that even Chloe didn't know, and Grace kept it that way deliberately. She had always disliked feeling stifled. As much as she loved her sister, there were times when she felt smothered by being half of an identical pair. She had her ways of rebelling, of breaking loose at times, but she kept that part of her life completely separate.

"Don't forget about your fitting tomorrow afternoon," Chloe reminded her as the two couples prepared to part after the meal.

Grace wrinkled her nose. "I don't know why I need to be measured and pinned and fussed over. Just try my dress on while you're being fitted for yours. If it fits you, we know it will fit me."

Chloe sighed. "I know you hate fittings, but it won't take long. You really do need to try the dress on yourself—just in case. Besides, you haven't even seen it. What if you don't like it?"

"It doesn't matter if I like it. It's your wedding. That gives you the right to choose the maid of honor's dress."

"You see how difficult she is?" Chloe complained to the men.

Grace watched as Bryan and Donovan exchanged a quizzical look. "Difficult?" Bryan asked tentatively. "She's letting you make all the decisions. That sounds pretty cooperative to me."

"Now *you're* being difficult," Chloe accused him with a shake of her head.

Bryan turned a questioning glance at Grace, who shrugged and mouthed, "Bridal jitters."

He seemed satisfied by that explanation.

Chapter Three

The long, busy day had left Grace tired, so that she was very quiet when Bryan took her home. He drove her in a car that had somehow become available to him at the restaurant. She no longer questioned how everything he needed seemed to simply materialize at his fingertips.

He lingered in the hallway outside her converted-loft apartment until she unlocked the door. She suspected courtesy suggested that she invite him in for a drink, but she really just wanted to be alone for now.

He seemed to sense her feelings. "Get some rest," he said. "I'll see you tomorrow."

She nodded and turned her doorknob. That might have been the end of the evening had the door to the stairwell at the end of the hallway not opened at that moment, accompanied by a burst of voices and laughter. Bryan seemed to react on sheer instinct, reaching out to pull her into his arms without any warning of his intentions. His mouth was on hers before she could ask what the heck he thought he was doing.

Maybe it was the element of surprise that kept her from resisting. Or maybe it was the awareness of those onlookers and the role she had agreed to play for the next few weeks. Telling herself this was only an act and Bryan was merely playing to their audience, she forced herself to relax and appear cooperative.

The problem was that it was all too easy to forget this was only an act. Whatever other problems she might have with him, Bryan Falcon certainly had a talent for clearing an otherwise intelligent woman's mind of all coherent thought.

The sounds of voices faded away as Bryan's mouth moved on hers.

Grace couldn't have said whether it was because the newcomers had stopped talking or her ears had simply stopped working. It seemed all she could concentrate on was the way his lips felt against hers, the strength of his arms around her, the warmth of his lean body as it pressed against hers. She found herself clutching his shirt, the expensive fabric gathered tightly in her fingers as she steadied herself. For some annoying reason, her legs were proving a bit unreliable at the moment.

She must be more tired than she had thought.

She pushed her heavy eyelids upward as Bryan slowly drew his lips away from hers. His gleaming midnight-blue eyes were very close to hers, their expression intense but impossible to interpret. Blinking to clear her vision, she glanced around the hallway to find that it was empty now, her neighbors having discreetly entered their own apartment.

Bryan's arms were still around her. She took a half-step backward, bumping against her apartment door. "Well…" she murmured, irked when her voice came out a croak. She cleared it quickly. "I guess that capped the performance for today."

Just a hint of a smile touched his lips. He dipped his head toward hers again. "How about an encore?"

Groping behind her with one hand, she quickly turned the doorknob, pushed the door open and moved another step backward. "Sorry. Final curtain."

With a good-natured smile, he straightened. "Good night, Grace."

She let herself into her apartment and closed the door behind her. And then she sagged against it, listening until Bryan's footsteps had faded away and the rumble of the elevator indicated he was gone.

"Elvis has left the building," she muttered, trying to find humor in a situation that had grown entirely too disconcerting.

Her lips were still tingling from his kiss, her stomach still fluttering like crazy. It had been a long time since she'd been involved with anyone—not since her engagement had ended a year ago, actually. Maybe, when this was all over, she should consider getting out more.

"Stand still, Grace. You're making it very difficult for Mrs. O'Neill to fit you."

"There's a straight pin sticking into my butt," Grace complained, squirming again.

The exasperated-looking, gray-haired woman

kneeling beside her made a hasty adjustment. "Is that better?"

"Some."

"Then why are you still wiggling?"

Grace made an effort to be still, even though she felt very much like a voodoo fashion doll being poked and prodded and peered at.

"You still haven't told me if you like the dress," Chloe reminded her from a few feet away in the fitting room of Ballew's Bridal Shoppe.

Glancing at the full-length mirror, Grace shrugged, dislodging a tiny waterfall of silver pins. Mrs. O'Neill grumbled something beneath her breath and gathered them up again. "The dress is fine. It's pretty."

And it was—a tasteful column of lavender silk accented with a diagonal sweep of rhinestones across the bodice. Pretty—but not a dress Grace would have chosen for herself. But it was Chloe's wedding, not hers, and the decisions were all Chloe's to make. Grace had no intention of arguing with any of them.

Which didn't mean she couldn't complain about a few other things. "Ouch!" she said as another sharp tip pricked her skin, this time at her waist.

Mrs. O'Neill finally scowled, the first time she had let her determinedly polite smile fade. "I *never* stick any of my clients with pins. But I rarely deal with anyone as wiggly and fidgety as you, either."

"Grace, *please* be still."

Grace exhaled gustily, then made a quick grab for the slipping strapless bodice of the still-unfitted gown. "Doesn't *anyone* wear sleeves anymore?"

With a show of severely strained patience, Mrs. O'Neill stuck another pin in the bodice to hold it in place. Grace had the feeling she'd just barely missed being stuck again—this time on purpose.

"I'm still, okay?" She struck a pose, facing the mirror. "I won't move another muscle."

Though she looked doubtful, Mrs. O'Neill went back to work quickly, perhaps trying to get as much accomplished as possible before Grace changed her mind.

Staying as motionless as she could, Grace studied the reflection of the slender woman in the sophisticated lavender dress. To keep it out of the way, she had twisted her hair up in the back, making her neck look longer and emphasizing her bare shoulders.

The woman in the mirror didn't look like Grace. She looked like Chloe.

"Are you almost finished?" she asked the seamstress. Her voice was strained with the effort of being still when what she really wanted to do was rip the lovely dress off and run naked for refuge.

"Yes." Mrs. O'Neill sounded almost as relieved as Grace felt. "You can change into your own clothes now. I'll leave your sister to help you. I—uh—have things to do in the other room."

Chloe stepped behind her twin to ease down the zipper hidden at the back of the dress. "I think you tried sweet Mrs. O'Neill's patience."

"She certainly tried mine. Those damned pins— I'm probably going to spring leaks next time I drink a glass of water."

"Oh, stop complaining. It's over now. And you looked gorgeous in the dress, by the way."

Grace tugged on the T-shirt and jeans she'd worn to the fitting and then pulled the clip from her hair.

She had to glance toward the mirror one more time just to make sure she was back to normal.

Chloe turned to hang the dress on a hook, close to the lacy white dress that hung nearby. Chloe had been fitted into that dress just prior to Grace's fitting. It was the dress their mother had worn in her wedding thirty-two years earlier. At five-six, Chloe and Grace were a couple of inches taller than their mother, which had necessitated the addition of a row of lace at the hem of the dress, taken from the mantilla-style veil their mother had worn. Other than that, Chloe wanted no changes made to the pretty, but very simple, gown.

It was going to be a sweet, unpretentious, lovely wedding, Grace mused. It suited Chloe perfectly.

Chloe sat on a tiny, padded chair to put on her shoes. Grace sat on the floor to fasten the straps of the heavy sandals she had worn. "So, how's it going with Bryan?" Chloe asked, keeping her voice very casual.

With a quick glance toward the closed door, Grace shrugged. "He's playing his part to the hilt," she murmured, mentally reliving that mind-scrambling good-night kiss.

"I'm still not entirely convinced this is necessary. It seems like you and Bryan are being terribly inconvenienced by…well, you know."

"It's no big deal," Grace bluffed. "Bryan seems to be getting a kick out of it all."

"He does have a rather odd sense of humor."

"No kidding. Anyway—it's been days since I've heard speculation that Donovan heartlessly stole you away from his best friend."

Chloe nodded to concede the point. "It has helped.

Even the ones who are suspicious about what really happened between Bryan and me are hesitant to openly talk about it now because they look foolish when we continue to deny it and refuse to be drawn into further discussion about it. And the society articles about your trip to New York referred to you repeatedly as Bryan's 'frequent companion,' which makes it sound like you've been seen together often.''

''I can handle being wined and dined for another few weeks. After that, life can get back to normal—for me, anyway.'' Even as she made the airy assertion, Grace knew life wouldn't be the same for either of them, really. Chloe would be married to a man whose career involved a lot of travel and perfunctory social obligations, though not as much of either as she would have faced had she married Bryan. Grace expected to find herself dealing with much more responsibility at the shop. She would be the one with no other obligations to interfere with the job.

Tugging at the neckline of her T-shirt, she asked, ''Is it hot in here to you? I can hardly breathe.''

''I'm almost ready.'' After checking her watch, Chloe stood in front of the mirror and ran her fingers through her short, tousled hair. In her khaki slacks and green-and-beige striped pullover, she looked neat and as fresh as if she'd just stepped out of a shower. Her own hair still disheveled from the clip, Grace felt rumpled and grubby next to her sister—as she often did.

She sighed impatiently when Chloe lingered to apply lipstick. ''We're going to your apartment, not to the theater. Would you c'mon, already?''

Chloe smiled as she put the lipstick away. ''Okay, so I'm primping because Donovan's picking us up. I know it doesn't matter to him if I'm wearing lipstick, considering he fell in love with me while we were lost in a forest, all torn and scraped and covered in mud. But I still like to look nice for him.''

Grace tried to smile, but it still angered her to think about the ordeal Chloe and Donovan had endured at the hands of their kidnappers. Grace had tried to talk Chloe out of leaving home that week; she'd had a bad feeling about it all along. Chloe had agreed to spend a week with Bryan at his luxurious vacation lodge in southern Missouri, with the specific intention of discussing the possibly of an old-fashioned marriage-of-convenience between them. Grace had been adamantly opposed to that plan, believing her sister deserved more than a calculated merger.

She'd been aware that Chloe's biological clock had been ticking wildly for some time, and apparently Bryan's had, too—or whatever the male equivalent could be called. But she *hadn't* agreed that compatible goals and dreams were enough to sustain a lifelong commitment. Besides which, she simply hadn't considered Bryan a good match for Chloe. She didn't know why—but every time she had seen Chloe and Bryan together…well, she simply hadn't liked it.

When Bryan had been delayed by business problems in New York, he had asked his trusted second-in-command, Donovan Chance, to escort Chloe to the lodge, where Bryan had hoped to join her quickly. Before he could do so, Chloe and Donovan had been snatched by three kidnappers, taken to an isolated forest hideaway and held for ransom until Donovan had orchestrated an escape into a million-acre forest. Several days of stormy weather and other daunting obstacles had slowed their rescue. For four days, Grace hadn't known where her sister was—or if she was even alive.

She shuddered with the memory of that horror. And she acknowledged—if only to herself—that Bryan had helped her through that time. He'd allowed her to vent her fear, her impatience, and her anger—and he'd given her strength by being calm, steady and ferocious in his determination to find his friends and the people who had taken them. When he'd uncovered evidence that one of his business competitors, Wallace Childers, had been the mastermind of the scheme, he had personally confronted Childers.

Watching the encounter, Grace had seen exactly how intimidating Bryan could be when he dropped the affable façade he wore in social situations. Childers had literally been in fear for his life when he'd reluctantly confessed everything—and Grace hadn't blamed the man for being concerned.

But Chloe was safe, she reminded herself with a glance at her twin's happy face. She had abandoned the foolish idea of a marriage-of-convenience in favor of a match based on true love. And Grace was doing her part to facilitate a happily-ever-after ending—for her sister, if not for herself.

Following Chloe out of the fitting room, she slung her oversized leather bag over her shoulder and muttered, "I still don't think it was necessary for Donovan to drive us here and pick us up. We're perfectly capable of getting around on our own."

"He wanted to," Chloe answered with a shrug. "He's still being a little overprotective, but that will change after the wedding. I'm afraid I'll have to insist on it."

Grace knew *she* would quickly grow tired of being

coddled and protected. She felt stifled enough now; being hovered over the way Donovan did Chloe would drive her nuts.

Which was why it was just as well she was single and unattached, she assured herself. She needed to be free. She wasn't the type to be tied down to any man. She'd learned that fact the hard way—with a wannabe cowboy named Kirk.

The sidewalks of Little Rock's River Market district were crowded late Tuesday morning as Bryan strolled toward the Pennington sisters' shop. Tuesdays and Saturdays were the area's busiest days during the summer. On those days, vendors gathered beneath the River Market pavilions to sell fresh produce, herbs, breads, flowers and other wares. Serving as a backdrop for the activities, the Arkansas River glittered with reflections of the bright July sun overhead. Locals and tourists in shorts and sandals ambled along the sidewalks, some carrying bulging bags of fresh fruits and veggies, others just window-shopping and enjoying the summer day.

A group of children in matching orange shirts emblazoned with the name of a local day care center dashed toward him, most likely headed toward the Museum of Discovery at the end of the block. Bryan sidestepped the chattering herd adroitly, nodding sympathetically to the adults trying to keep them under control.

He paused to study a grouping of paintings displayed on the sidewalk next to the River Market building, which housed several food stands and restaurants and gift shops. The artist, a striking black woman in a flowing dress and a big straw hat, had chosen vivid colors for her scenes of tropical marketplaces and fishing villages. One canvas in particular caught his attention. He stood in front of it for several minutes, enjoying the colors and the overall impression of cheery, bustling activity. It reminded him of his favorite marketplace in Jamaica; he could almost hear the lilting voices and the street musicians in the background.

Ten minutes later, he was on his way again, having left directions with the artist to have his newly purchased painting delivered to his Little Rock office. Bryan wasn't usually an impulse buyer, but he knew what he liked when he saw it, and he was fortunate enough to be able to afford what he liked.

Yet all that money hadn't helped him find anyone with whom to share his interests. In fact, it had proven a definite hindrance, drawing too much attention to his tentative relationships, and raising doubts about the true motives of the women who had shown an interest in him.

Chiding himself for letting such maudlin thoughts shadow his enjoyment of the nice day, he crossed the street toward the entrance of Mirror Images. Big windows on either side of the door were artfully arranged with uniquely shaped mirrors, framed prints, unusual candlesticks and other decorative wares. The display had drawn its share of attention; several potential customers were milling in the shop when Bryan entered. In response to the chime of the bell above the door, Chloe approached with a polite smile that warmed when she recognized him. "Good morning, Bryan."

It was easier to tell the twins apart now that Chloe had cut her hair differently—not that Bryan had ever had much trouble recognizing them. Their personalities were so different that he had usually been able to distinguish them by their expressions alone. He took Chloe's outstretched hand. "Good morning. You look beautiful, as always."

"And you're as full of blarney as usual," she retorted, though she looked pleased by the compliment. "What's up?"

"I had a rare couple of hours free this morning and I thought I'd pop in for a visit. If I'm not interfering with your work, of course."

"Of course not. Justin can handle the sales floor for a few minutes," Chloe replied with a nod toward her salesclerk. "He'll call for me if he needs help. Come have a glass of tea with me in my office."

Aware of the attention they were receiving from her customers, he accepted promptly. "I would love to."

The small office Chloe shared with her sister never failed to elicit a grin from Bryan. Chloe's side of the room was neat, organized, not a sheet of paper out of place; Grace's desk was so cluttered it was a wonder she could find her chair. Above Chloe's desk hung a framed museum poster of a Monet water lilies painting. Grace's poster depicted a fiery red Corvette convertible. She'd told him once that she dreamed of owning such a vehicle someday. Bryan had impulsively offered to buy her one as compensation for her inconveniences because of his scheme to take media attention from Chloe and Donovan. Grace had let him know in clear and concise terms that she would fulfill her own dreams, thank you very much.

His amusement turning wry with the memory, he asked casually, "Where is Grace?"

"It was her turn to run errands—the bank, the post office, the office supplies store."

Bryan wouldn't admit to Chloe, of course, that he'd been disappointed that Grace wasn't there when he arrived. It was disconcerting enough to acknowledge to himself that it was Grace who had drawn him here today. "How's she holding up?" he asked. "With the scam we're pulling off, I mean."

Chloe wrinkled her nose as she removed a plastic pitcher of tea from the small refrigerator in one corner of the crowded room. "She fusses about it, of course, but Grace does love to fuss."

He chuckled. "I've noticed."

"And she is *not* happy that one of your men is following at a discreet distance while she runs her errands."

"Tough. Fussing won't do her any good when it comes to her security—not while I have anything to say about it, anyway."

Grace poured tea into two glasses she had removed from a cabinet above the minifridge. "Daddy used to call us Sissy and Sassy. I was Sissy, of course."

"Of course."

"Anyway, he stopped calling us that when we were about twelve. Grace threatened to run away if he didn't."

"And, knowing her, she would have followed through on that threat."

"Daddy must have thought so. He dropped the nicknames."

There had been a time when Bryan had considered Grace's mercurial, temperamental tendencies annoying. Yet the better he got to know her, the more he enjoyed being with her. And the better he understood her. If from early childhood she had been known as the "difficult" twin, it was certainly understandable that she'd gotten into the habit of living up to the reputation.

There was something else, too. Some hidden part of Grace that he hadn't quite figured out yet. He was becoming more determined all the time to try.

"What about you?" Chloe asked, handing him his glass of iced tea. "Are you growing tired of the charade yet? You know, of course, that you can stop anytime if it's becoming too uncomfortable for you. You've already diffused a great deal of the gossip that was upsetting Donovan so badly a few weeks ago."

"True—but there's no need to risk having it resurface before your wedding. Besides, I'm rather enjoying keeping the tattle mongers guessing."

"I know you love playing practical jokes, especially on the tabloid writers, but you're spending a lot of time with my sister—who, you have to admit, has not been your biggest fan in the past and isn't shy about expressing her feelings."

He sipped his tea, then spoke lightly. "I don't mind spending time with Grace. She's certainly...challenging."

Chloe laughed. "She is that. Grace is rarely boring, you have to give her that."

"Grace is *never* boring," he corrected with a smile.

Studying him speculatively over the rim of her glass, she murmured, "You sound as though you're starting to like my sister."

"Of course I like your sister. I've always liked her—even when she fantasized about hiring some big, beefy guy named Vinnie to make me conveniently disappear from your life."

Chloe giggled. ''Now you're exaggerating. She was simply concerned that we were acting impulsively when we discussed the possibility of marriage—and it turned out she was right. You know full well that you would have changed your mind if I hadn't. You probably had already changed your mind, but you were polite enough to let me be the one to put it into words.''

Bryan had asked himself several times if he would have actually married Chloe had she not fallen in love with Donovan. It had seemed like a good idea; they had both been eager to find partners and have children. He had finally convinced himself that a marriage of minds, rather than emotions, was the only solution. Maybe his background had left him unprepared for anything else.

His own parents' marriage had been a profitable merger between two business dynasties. Once they'd done their duty and produced an heir, they'd been more than happy to pretty much go their own ways. Divorce had never been an option; since neither interfered with the other, there'd been no need to put an end to their partnership. The marriage had actually been a convenient excuse for both of them, since neither had been interested in marrying again. Bryan had grown up knowing that his parents were quite fond of him, in their own busy, distracted ways, and tolerated each other when it was socially necessary.

The telephone on Chloe's desk rang suddenly, interrupting his reminiscences. She answered with her professional voice, but then her tone warmed. Bryan knew immediately who was on the other end of the line. He'd never seen Chloe react this way to anyone but Donovan.

She'd never felt even remotely the same way about *him*.

"I can leave as soon as Grace returns," he heard her say into the phone. "It should be no more than half an hour."

Bryan stood, intending to leave her to finish her call in privacy, but she stopped him with a motion of her hand. "I'll see you in half an hour," she told her fiancé, then disconnected the call.

"Donovan just called to see if I'm free for lunch," she explained to Bryan after returning the receiver to its cradle. "You don't have to rush off."

He remained on his feet. "I've kept you from your work long enough. I just wanted to say hello. Thanks for the tea."

She rose and moved closer to him, smiling. "I enjoyed the visit. I have always considered you a good friend, Bryan. I'm glad we've been able to maintain that relationship."

"I will always be your friend," he replied immediately. "And since the man you're marrying is like a brother to me, we're almost family now."

Her smile deepened prettily. "I like that."

"So do I." Feeling rather as if he was officially sealing the new status of their relationship, he leaned over to brush a kiss against her cheek.

"Sorry. Am I interrupting?"

Grace's dry question drew their attention toward the doorway. Chloe had left the door partially ajar, so neither she nor Bryan had heard Grace push it open. She stood in the doorway now with her hands on her hips and her eyes narrowed as she looked from him to Chloe and back again.

Moving a step away from Chloe, Bryan nodded. "Hello, Grace. How's it going?"

"Fine. Chloe, Justin needs you at the counter. Something about a special order for Mrs. Crothers?"

"Oh, right. I'll go take care of that before Donovan comes to take me to lunch."

Still giving Bryan a look that made him feel as though he should shuffle his feet and apologize for something—anything—Grace moved out of her sister's way. She stepped back into the doorway before Bryan could follow Chloe out. "What are you doing here?"

"It's nice to see you, too. You look lovely, by the way. I've always liked you in green."

Grace's reaction to his flattery was just the opposite of her sister's. She seemed to grow even more suspicious of him. "You didn't answer my question."

"Why am I here? I had a couple hours free—okay, actually I ducked a meeting that seemed both pointless and much too boring for such a nice day. I took a walk through the River Market district and ended up here. Chloe poured tea for me and we had a nice chat. Would you like a transcript of our conversation?"

She didn't respond to the lame jest except to glare even harder. "It doesn't look right—you kissing my sister when she's engaged to someone else."

"Jealous?" he shot back, holding on to his patience with an effort.

Her cheeks flamed—a response he found quite interesting. "Don't be a jackass, Bryan. I'm just thinking about what the gossip columnists would write if someone reported to them that you were kissing Chloe in her office. The whole point of this game we're all playing is to defuse any talk about you and my sister, remember?''

"It was a friendly peck on the cheek between friends, nothing more. No one saw us except you— and I doubt you're going to alert the media. And I'm tired of standing here defending my actions to you. So, if you'll excuse me, I have things to do."

She moved slowly out of his way as he approached. ''I simply…''

He didn't want to hear any more lecturing from her at the moment. "See you around, Grace," he said.

On an impulse, he stopped in front of her and reached out to thread his fingers into her hair. He covered her mouth with his before she could guess his intentions. "Report *that* to the media," he murmured after he released her, then turned and made a hasty exit.

Chapter Four

Grace wished she could spend Thursday evening scrubbing floors. Or paying bills. Even cleaning bathrooms seemed preferable to yet another evening socializing with the rich and semifamous.

This time it was a political fund-raiser at an exclusive Little Rock country club. The governor would be there, along with a gaggle of other politicians, several notable business leaders, a few sports heroes and Arkansas-born celebrities, and a military dignitary or two. Grace figured she would be as out of place there as a cat at a dog show, but she had made a commitment and she wouldn't back out—no matter how badly she might want to.

Dressed in a sleeveless black silk dress—her limited wardrobe was going to force her to go shopping soon if she had to keep attending these glitzy events—she entered the ballroom at Bryan's side. It had been somewhat awkward between them so far. Bryan was in one of his annoying, teasing-and-flirting moods, and she was still sulking over that parting kiss Tuesday in her office. He'd left her sputtering for a snappy comeback and mentally kicking herself for not physically kicking *him*. And he'd probably guessed everything she was thinking, the jerk.

Conversations in the ballroom were discreetly muted, with only an occasional burst of laughter here and there. An orchestra played elevator-suitable show tunes, and unrecognizable, but probably very expensive, hors d'oeuvres were artfully arranged on tables decorated with candles and ice sculptures—a potentially unfortunate combination, in Grace's opinion.

Everyone in the room seemed to be on a first-name basis with Bryan—including the governor. They spent what seemed like a few days circling the room, swapping greetings and meaningless pleasantries and incredibly lame jokes.

"You can stop smiling now," Bryan murmured when they had paused in a dim corner after making the obligatory rounds. "No one's looking."

"No," she snapped back, "I can't. My face is permanently stuck in this stupid expression. It's going to be like this for the rest of my life, and then I'm going to die and lie in my coffin grinning inanely at all the mourners who pass by."

He laughed and looped an arm around her shoulders. "Don't worry, darling. I'm sure I'll do something to wipe the smile from your face soon."

"Watch that roving hand," she growled.

He laughed again and moved his hand to a more innocuous position. "What did I tell you?"

"Can we leave yet?"

"Darling, we just got here."

"It feels as if we've been here for a week. And do you *have* to call me darling every ten seconds or so?"

"Of course not. Sweetheart."

Because punching one's escort in the stomach was considered impolite, and because she had made a vow to herself to be on her best behavior that evening, Grace decided to let that one pass.

She happened to be looking at Bryan when his smile suddenly froze, then slowly faded. "Well, hell."

Her left eyebrow rose. "What's wrong?"

"My parents just walked in."

Turning to follow the direction of his gaze, she tried to spot a likely looking couple among the well-dressed crowd. She'd never met Bryan's parents, and he rarely spoke of them, at least to her. "I take it you weren't expecting them?"

"I thought Dad was on a fishing trip in Belize."

He didn't seem particularly pleased to find out otherwise. Grace turned to study his expression, which was difficult to read. "You don't get along with your parents?"

With a slight shrug, he replied, "We get along fine. Dad's still a little annoyed with me for leaving the family business to go off on my own, but he rather enjoys the bragging rights that go along with my success. My mother has always had a fascination with celebrities, so she's always nagging me to introduce her to movie stars and supermodels—even the ones I've never met. She knows everyone in the local social community, of course, but she's always fantasized about mingling with the Hollywood elite— something my father couldn't care less about."

"Maybe you should have brought one of your starlet girlfriends tonight—for your mother's sake."

He responded to her flippant quip with a scowl. "I don't happen to have any 'starlet girlfriends' at the moment."

"I doubt that would have proven much of a handicap to you. I'm sure there are numbers you could call…"

Something glittered in his eyes that might have been a warning, but his smile didn't waver when he said, "Why would I want to be here with anyone else but you, *darling?*"

Before she could answer, a woman's voice crooned, "There you are, Bryan. I wasn't sure we'd see you here this evening."

Grace looked around curiously, studying the couple who had approached them. She knew their names—Richard and Judith Falcon. They were an attractive couple, as she might have expected, considering Bryan's extraordinary good looks. She assumed they were in their mid-sixties, but both were in excellent condition. Richard was tall and straight, his silvered hair swept back from a tanned and strong-planed face. Bryan had inherited his bone structure and his piercing blue eyes from his father, Grace decided, but his charming smile had come straight from his mother.

Slender to the point of angularity and a couple of inches taller than Grace, Judith had kept her hair a dark auburn, worn in short waves around a carefully made-up face that bore few lines. Grace suspected that this was a woman on very close terms with at least one cosmetic surgeon, but she couldn't deny that the efforts had paid off. Judith certainly didn't look old enough to have a son who was pushing forty.

"Actually I'm surprised to see the two of you here," Bryan said in answer to his mother's greeting. "Dad, I thought you were in Belize. And, Mom, weren't you going to France with a group of your friends?"

"My fishing trip fell through," Richard explained. "Bob Wheatley had a heart attack last week. Since the reservations were in his name, Steve and I decided it would be better to cancel than to try to rearrange everything."

It seemed to Grace that he was more irked by the inconvenience of changing his plans than concerned about his acquaintance's health. Maybe Bryan was thinking along the same lines when he murmured, "I'm sorry to hear about your friend's illness. I trust he's recovering?"

"Oh, sure, he'll be okay. The doctors did a couple of bypasses and they'll be sending him home in a couple of days."

"And what about your trip to France, Mother?"

"That's been rescheduled until next month because of a problem with the tour service." Apparently losing interest in the conversation, Judith glanced at Grace then. "I'm sorry, we're being rude. You must be Chloe."

Bryan sighed. "This is Grace, Mother. Chloe is her sister, who's engaged to Donovan."

"Yes, of course." Judith didn't seem at all embarrassed by her gaffe as she touched her fingers to Grace's hand. "An understandable mistake, of course. The columnists linked your name with Chloe's for several months before you corrected them about which twin you're actually seeing."

"I've warned you against believing everything you read about me in the tabloids."

Her smile was tight-lipped. "How else am I supposed to find out about your social life? *You* certainly never tell me anything."

"He probably doesn't consider his personal life any more your business than the gossip columnists'," Richard said bluntly. And then he nodded toward Grace. "Nice to meet you. Now if you'll excuse me, I need to have a word with the senator."

Grace had seen more warmth between Bryan and his business associates than he'd shared with his father. She looked at him through her lashes, wondering if his relationship with his parents had always been so strained.

Judith spoke to her son again after her husband moved away without a backward glance at her. "Have you seen that lovely young actress lately, Bryan? The one who won the Academy Award. She seems so nice."

He pulled Grace closer to his side. "She didn't win the award, Mother, she was only nominated. And I haven't seen her—or anyone else—since Grace and I got together."

"I see." She eyed Grace speculatively. "Are you originally from Little Rock? Do I know your family?"

"No, I grew up in Searcy. My parents still live there."

"Oh? What do your parents do?"

"My mother's a schoolteacher. My father sells insurance."

"I see." And she couldn't have been less impressed.

Bryan's arm tightened around Grace's waist. His voice was terse when he spoke. "Grace and her sister co-own a decorating accessories shop in the River Market district. They're quite popular with local decorators because they carry such an interesting selection of mirrors and other unique items. You would probably love it."

"We call the shop 'Mirror Images,'" Grace added, feeling a need to help him keep the conversation moving.

"I must make a point to drop in sometime."

"I would love for you to do so," Grace lied in reply.

"Oh, there's the first lady. Dreadful color she's wearing, isn't it? Ah, well…excuse me, I have to go speak with her. Her feelings will be hurt if I don't."

"Actually I think the poor woman would be relieved," Bryan murmured into Grace's ear. "My mother is a snob, but she's not as bad as the first impression she gives."

"I have a feeling she would have been friendlier if I had an Oscar on my mantel," she answered wryly.

"She's just sulking because I haven't kept her up-to-date on who I'm seeing, and that keeps her out of the gossip loop. I never discussed Chloe with her because I didn't want to talk about my plans until Chloe and I had a chance to get to know each other."

What he meant, Grace decided, was that he hadn't wanted to mention Chloe until he knew whether she was going to marry him. "So your own mother doesn't know for certain that you were dating Chloe before she met Donovan?"

"No," he said with a quick glance around to make

sure she hadn't been overheard. "And neither will anyone else—unless you broadcast it tonight."

Fully aware that no one was close enough to overhear, Grace only shrugged. "I suppose you haven't told your parents why you're now taking pains to be seen with me?"

"No. I saw no reason to discuss that with them, either."

"So they probably believe what they hear through the grapevine—that you and I are involved in a serious relationship."

The discussion seemed to be making him increasingly nervous. He was standing so close to her that she spoke almost directly into his ear; an eavesdropper would almost have to be standing between them to overhear. To everyone else, it probably appeared that they were engaged in an intimate conversation. Still, Bryan made it clear that he'd rather not talk about their relationship—or lack of one—under those conditions. "Would you like to dance?"

"Not particularly."

"Great. Let's go."

She stifled a sigh and allowed herself to be towed to the dance floor.

The one redeeming aspect of the fund-raiser, in Grace's opinion, was Bryan's dancing talent. Despite her initial rejection of his offer, she loved to dance, and wasn't able to do so very often. It was nice to have a skilled partner who seemed to enjoy the activity as much as she did.

They danced the rest of the evening away. Maybe it was because Bryan was trying to avoid further stilted conversation with his parents—or trying to spare Grace from the chore. Or maybe it was the novelty of finding something they could enjoy together without the underlying friction that usually existed between them. They even laughed together while they experimented with intricate dance steps. And when the movements brought them close, their bodies brushing as they moved slowly to some blatantly romantic arrangement...well, that was nice, too.

A bit *too* nice, as far as Grace was concerned. She had to keep reminding herself not to confuse make-believe with reality.

"You never told me you were such a good dancer," Bryan murmured into her ear as the orchestra played a sultry rendition of "Misty."

"Should I have included dancing on my personal résumé for you?"

He chuckled, making his chest vibrate pleasantly against her. "I have a feeling there are several tidbits on that résumé that I would find interesting."

"I doubt that mine would be half as interesting as yours."

"Maybe we'll compare notes someday."

She decided to let that suggestion pass.

Looking over his shoulder, she said, instead, "I see that your father is dancing with the senator's wife."

A muscle twitched in Bryan's jaw. "Is he?"

"You find that surprising?"

"Not really. My father has always had a knack for staying on friendly terms with his exes. Too bad I didn't inherit the talent—my relationships always seem to crash and burn."

"You and Chloe have certainly remained good friends."

"But Chloe and I were never involved in what you

would call a real relationship," he reminded her in a murmur.

Because other couples were dancing nearby, she said no more about her sister, asking instead, "So your father dated the senator's wife before he married your mother?"

Bryan lifted an eyebrow. "That's an uncharacteristically naive comment, coming from you. That lovely lady was still in junior high when my parents married."

"Oh." She looked again at the attractive blonde dancing with Richard Falcon, and felt foolish for not immediately realizing the truth.

"My parents have a very modern and sophisticated marriage," Bryan added dispassionately. "Discreet dalliances are allowed—even encouraged—as long as they're conducted quietly and carefully."

Grace gave Bryan a hard look. "If that's what your family considers a marriage, I'm even more relieved that Chloe met Donovan."

"I said it was my parents' idea of marriage, not mine."

She thought about that as the music ended and they moved a few steps apart. Bryan implied that he wanted a more traditional marriage than what his parents had, and yet he'd never pretended to be in love with Chloe, even when he proposed to her. He'd described a marriage based on friendship, affection, a mutual desire for children—but romance had nothing to do with it.

From what she'd seen of his parents, it was no wonder he was confused about what a real marriage was supposed to be. She thought of her own parents, who had recently celebrated their thirtieth wedding anniversary. They had married for love and had kept the promises they'd made to each other through good times and the inevitable hard times. And they were still the best of friends.

That was the type of marriage Grace wanted for Chloe and Donovan. It was what she had hoped for when she'd become engaged to Kirk—until she'd belatedly realized that *his* idea of a wife was someone who stood on the sidelines cheering him on. Someone who catered to his every whim, and made herself over to suit him. Grace had found herself incapable of becoming that person—not even to please the man she'd thought she loved.

"All this dancing has made me thirsty," Bryan commented. "Why don't I find us a couple of glasses of champagne?"

She nodded. "I'd like to freshen up a bit. I'll rejoin you in a few minutes."

His wicked smile made a sudden reappearance when he caught her hand and lifted it to his lips. "I'll be counting the moments until you're with me again. Hurry back, darling."

She sighed. "Stuff it in your ear, Falcon."

His low laugh followed her as she turned and marched away.

She was standing in front of a gilt-framed mirror in the crystal-and-marble appointed ladies' lounge, a tube of lipstick in her hand, when a tall brunette approached her. "You're here with Bryan Falcon, aren't you?"

After recapping the lipstick, Grace dropped the tube into her tiny black evening bag. "Yes, I am."

"I'm Katherine Stanley."

"Grace Pennington. Are you a friend of Bryan's?"

"Oh, no. I don't travel in his circles. I'm a financial reporter for the state newspaper. I've written quite a bit about his business ventures, and I met him once at a business seminar, but I doubt that he would even remember me."

"You might be surprised. Bryan has a phenomenal memory for names and faces." Especially, Grace would guess, if the face in question was this pretty.

Katherine shrugged modestly. "Perhaps. Anyway…what's it like being involved with a man like Bryan Falcon?"

Grace concentrated on fastening the clasp of her purse. "I, um…"

"Oh, I'm not angling for gossip to print in my column. That's not what I write. I'm afraid I simply let curiosity overcome good manners."

Grace gave the other woman a slight smile. "I'm getting used to that, I guess. Bryan seems to arouse a great deal of curiosity."

Katherine nodded, then broke into a rueful grin. "You have to admit the man is flat-out dazzling."

Grace laughed softly. "Okay, I'll give you that."

"It must be difficult for you—being the center of so much attention, reading all that silly tabloid gossip about whether Bryan was dating your sister before you."

"It does get tiresome." With one last glance in the mirror, Grace turned toward the door. "Nice to meet you, Katherine."

The other woman spoke quickly. "You might mention to Mr. Falcon that you met me. I would love to interview him for the financial section sometime. No gossip, just straight business talk."

Grace shrugged and motioned toward the door. "Come ask him yourself."

Looking suddenly nervous, the reporter cleared her throat. "You mean now?"

"He's here, you're here. Why not now?"

"Well, I, um…"

Grace had never expected to meet a shy reporter. Apparently Katherine Stanley had used up her courage by introducing herself to Grace. "Don't worry. I'm sure he'll be pleased to see you again."

If there was one thing she could guarantee about Bryan, it was that he was unfailingly gracious in social situations. Even if he preferred not to be interviewed for Katherine's newspaper, he would decline politely. He might be surprised that Grace was helping a reporter after she'd been so careful to avoid them lately, but Katherine was hardly a tabloid tattle monger. Grace rather liked this one.

Bryan had commandeered a small table. He waited there with two flutes of champagne and a dessert plate of chocolate-dipped strawberries—one of Grace's favorite treats. He rose when he spotted Grace and her newfound companion.

Plucking a strawberry from the plate, Grace said, "Bryan, this is Katherine Stanley. She's a financial reporter."

Flashing one of his patented smiles, Bryan took the other woman's hand. "Yes, we've met. It was at that Arkansas investors' seminar last spring, wasn't it?"

The young woman seemed stunned that he had recognized her, even though Grace had predicted that he would. "Yes, my editor introduced us in passing."

"Would you like some champagne?"

"No, thank you. I have to get back to my friends.

I met Ms. Pennington in the ladies' lounge, and when I mentioned that I would like to do an interview with you sometime about your latest business ventures, she invited me to accompany her.''

Bryan glanced at Grace, who was thoroughly enjoying the biggest, sweetest strawberry she'd ever tasted and pretending not to listen to his conversation with the reporter. ''My schedule's rather full at present, but I'm sure I can make time for a brief interview. Call my office next week and talk to my assistant. I'll tell her to expect your call.''

Visibly delighted, Katherine thanked him, and then thanked Grace. ''It was so nice to see you both. I think you make a great couple,'' she added artlessly as she turned to rush away.

Bryan lifted his champagne flute to Grace in a minisalute. ''To us—a great couple.''

''A compatible team,'' she amended, ''at least for now.''

She sipped the champagne, telling herself she would be glad when there was no further need for this temporary partnership. And trying very hard to believe it.

Chapter Five

Despite her perfunctory assertion that there was no need for him to walk her all the way to her door, Bryan escorted Grace to her apartment after the fundraiser. He hadn't forgotten the last time they had stood outside this door, when the sudden appearance of her neighbors had generated an impulsive goodnight kiss between them. Judging from Grace's posture, she hadn't forgotten, either.

He'd thought of that kiss—and the reasons behind it—several times since that night. True enough, they'd agreed to keep up the charade of an intimate relationship whenever outside observers were around. Her neighbors would have expected him to kiss her before leaving her for the evening. And yet, he was fully aware that he'd wanted to kiss her then, and had seized the first excuse to do so.

He wanted to kiss her again now.

"I had a very nice time with you tonight," he said, testing her mood in the elevator.

She blinked a couple of times, as if the sound of his voice had roused her from deep thought. "I, um, what did you say?"

Wondering what she'd been pondering so intently, he repeated his comment.

"Oh. Well, the evening wasn't as bad as I expected. I enjoyed the dancing."

It wasn't exactly a glowing endorsement of the event, but coming from Grace, it was close. "I was a bit surprised that you brought a reporter to our table."

"I kind of liked her. Besides, she's a real reporter, not one of those sleazy tabloid writers. Maybe if the media starts concentrating on your business ventures again, they'll stop focusing so intently on your private life."

"I agree. Most of that attention came from the 'America's Most Eligible Bachelors' article that was published last year. It was right after that absurd list that gossip started going around that I was seriously seeing someone here in Little Rock, thinking about getting married, maybe. Now that so many of the columnists are feeling foolish because they can't say with absolute certainty which twin I met and dated first, they've almost stopped saying anything at all about me."

"Great," she said a bit too heartily as the elevator doors slid open. "Then we've accomplished what we set out to do."

He followed close behind her down the hallway toward her apartment. "That's true—but we don't want to abruptly stop seeing each other now, especially not before the wedding. That could start the gossip all over again.''

She sighed. ''I guess you're right,'' she conceded grudgingly.

''So...what next? Do you have any upcoming social events at which we could be seen together?''

''I have no social events,'' she replied, shoving her key into the lock of her door.

''I've noticed that you haven't talked much about your life away from your shop. Other than dancing, what do you like to do for fun?''

''Oh, this and that. Good night, Bryan.''

She'd slipped inside her door as soon as she opened it, and would have closed it in his face had he not reached out to block it. ''I wouldn't mind a cup of coffee, if it isn't too much trouble.''

She frowned. ''Well, I...''

''We need to talk about our plans for the next couple of weeks,'' he added. ''While we have a chance to talk in private, I mean.''

Hesitating only another moment, she nodded and held the door open for him.

''I really do like your apartment,'' he remarked, masking his satisfaction that she had allowed him inside. He wandered across the big, open main room to gaze out the window that dominated the back wall of her living room. Reflections of the moon and the city lights glittered like diamonds scattered across the black satin surface of the Arkansas River. The apartment itself was rather modest, containing the living room, an eat-in kitchen, a single bedroom and bath— maybe eight hundred square feet total—but the view was impressive.

''Thanks. I like it, too. Chloe prefers the suburban

setting of west Little Rock, but I like being downtown. It's been interesting watching the area transform itself from a row of dilapidated, abandoned warehouses to a thriving neighborhood filled with shops, galleries, museums, restaurants and breweries. I'm close to the main library and the Arkansas Repertory Theater, and the Alltel Arena is just across the river, so I can easily attend concerts and sporting events such as hockey and arena football.''

He knew all this, of course, being a Little Rock native, himself. He could only assume she was babbling because it made her nervous to be alone with him in her apartment.

She must have realized what she was doing at the same time he did. ''I'll make the coffee,'' she said and hurried into the kitchen.

He moved to sit on the couch, his attention lingering for a moment on the intriguely shaped pottery pieces arranged on her glass-topped coffee table. Trying to find hints of her other interests, he looked around the colorfully decorated room, paying particular notice to a built-in bookcase crowded with an eclectic assortment of paperback novels and movies on DVD. Did she spend all her free hours alone here in her apartment, reading and watching films? That didn't seem to mesh with what he knew of her, yet he saw no evidence to the contrary.

He knew Chloe had interests outside of work; she enjoyed volunteering through several community service organizations and she had been taking pottery classes at the Arkansas Arts Center. He wondered if the pieces on Grace's table included any of Chloe's work. Chloe also enjoyed fly-fishing and traveling, two of the mutual pastimes that Bryan had considered a sign that he and Chloe had a great deal in common.

But Grace was still a mystery to him. Chloe had chatted openly about herself during their few discreet dinner dates; Grace had revealed almost nothing to him. He'd learned only this evening how much she enjoyed dancing, for example.

He wondered why she was so reticent about revealing anything of herself to him. Was it because she didn't expect to spend much time with him after Chloe and Donovan married? Or did she simply dislike him so much that she didn't want him to know much about her?

If it was the latter, he'd have to see what he could do to change her attitude toward him. He had grown rather spoiled to having other people—of both genders—like and respect him, and he was well aware of that small conceit. But why *wouldn't* she like him? He was a nice guy. Good company. A more than decent dancer. He wasn't trying to charm her into falling desperately in love with him, of course, but he would like to think they could become friends in addition to reluctant co-conspirators.

She carried two mugs of coffee when she rejoined him. Handing him his mug, she settled into a chair with her own, eyeing him somewhat warily over the rim. "What do you want to talk about?"

He certainly had his work cut out for him. For whatever reason, she didn't trust him entirely. That was a problem he would have to overcome before they could establish any sort of friendship, even a casual one. "The wedding is still three weeks away. I think we should probably be seen publicly together two or three more times prior to the wedding, and then a few more times afterward before we drop the pretense. Just to be on the safe side. Do you agree?''

''I suppose you're right.''

He might have wished for a little more enthusiasm, but he would settle for what he could get. ''So far we've only been seen together at events that are related to my business dealings. Don't you think we would be more believable as a couple if you introduce me to some of *your* friends? Don't you have a party or a bowling team or something we can attend together?''

''A bowling team?''

He shrugged. ''Just an example.''

''No, I don't belong to a bowling team.''

''No upcoming parties? Club meetings? Business-related social functions?''

She kept her gaze focused on her coffee. ''My calendar is fairly clear at the moment. I'm open to your suggestions about things we can do together.''

He had plenty of suggestions, but he doubted that many of them would appeal to her at the moment. Since she seemed to have no intention of voluntarily sharing her life with him, it looked as though it was up to him to keep trying to come up with ideas. ''What do you like to do for fun? If not bowling, I mean.''

She shrugged. ''Lots of things. Nothing in particular.''

She was one of the most elusive women he had ever met. Getting a straight answer from her was like trying to grab a handful of smoke. ''I know you work Saturday, but are you free Sunday?''

''I can be.''

He nodded. ''Then I'll pick you up Sunday morning around ten o'clock. Dress very casually. Comfortably.''

"Where are we going?"

He hadn't a clue—but he was sure he would come up with something. "I'll surprise you."

If she had looked nervous before, she appeared doubly so now. "Um…"

He flashed her a grin. "You trust me, don't you?"

"Not as far as I can throw you," she answered without hesitation.

He laughed and set his empty mug aside. "It's getting late. I'd better go."

She sprang to her feet and hurried to the door as if anxious to see him out. "I'll see you Sunday."

"You could try to sound a little more enthusiastic," he said as he moved toward her.

"I said I would cooperate with this plan, and I will. You think we should be seen together a few more times for Chloe and Donovan's sake. I'll take your word for it."

"Very noble and self-sacrificing of you."

A light blush tinted her fair cheeks. "There's no reason for you to make fun of me."

"I'm only teasing." He paused in front of her to stroke her flushed cheek with his fingertips. "Chloe is very lucky to have you for a sister."

Her color deepened. "She would do the same for me."

"Yes, I know. You're lucky to have each other."

"You're doing all this for Donovan," she reminded him.

"Of course. But it hasn't really been such a hardship for me to spend time with you. I've enjoyed it, actually."

The compliment only made her frown deepen. "Um...thank you. I guess."

Shaking his head, he feigned a sigh. "Even if you *are* rough on my ego," he added in a mutter.

She narrowed her eyes at him. "Bolstering your ego was not part of the deal."

"True. But you can't blame a guy for wishing."

She put a hand on the doorknob. "Good night, Bryan."

He slid his hand around to her nape, leaning closer to her.

He didn't manage to catch her off guard this time. She jumped away from him as if she were avoiding an electric shock, her scowl warning him off. "There's no one watching us now. That isn't necessary."

"Practice?" he suggested hopefully.

She shook her head. "You hardly need any practice."

Giving her a resigned smile, he said, "I'll take that as a compliment. Thanks."

She opened the door. "Go away, Bryan. You're giving me a headache."

"You'd better stock up on aspirin. I'm going to be around for a while."

As her door closed behind him, he thought he heard her mutter, "That's what I'm afraid of."

He was chuckling when he headed for the elevator—and looking forward to Sunday.

"...and I thought Mother was going to hyperventilate when Mrs. Cochran said a conflict had come up for the photographer on the day of the wedding. Honestly, you would think Mother was the bride. I said,

'Mom, calm down. There are plenty of other photographers.' And she said, 'Yes, but he's the best and we want the best.' So I... Grace, are you listening? Grace?''

The sound of her own name brought Grace out of her thoughts. Realizing that she'd been standing in the same spot for quite a while, a palm-sized, brass-framed mirror in her hand, she set the mirror on a shelf and said, ''I'm listening. You said you aren't going to get to use the photographer you wanted?''

Chloe shook her head. ''That's the part I was about to tell you. The conflict was settled and everything worked out.''

''Oh. That's great.''

''I can tell you're beside yourself with excitement.'' Chloe set a feather duster on the sales counter and moved to stand in front of her twin, her hands planted on her hips. ''What's going on, Grace?''

''Nothing.''

''Don't give me that. Something's been bothering you all day. Did anything happen between you and Bryan last night?''

Busying herself with making sure the Closed sign was in place and the front door was securely locked, Grace answered gruffly, ''Everything was fine last night. We danced a lot. You know I enjoy dancing.''

''Well, yes. And Bryan's a wonderful dancer.''

Grace looked over her shoulder. ''You've danced with him?''

''He took me dancing a couple of times when we were...well, you know.''

''Dating,'' Grace supplied in a mutter.

''Spending time together,'' Chloe corrected. ''Before I met Donovan, of course.''

Grace didn't need to be reminded that the main reason Chloe and Bryan had stopped "spending time together" was that Chloe had fallen in love with someone else. Bryan would probably be quite content to still be dancing with Chloe.

Grace was well aware that she was a temporary substitute in Bryan's life. After the wedding, she and Bryan would go their own ways, seeing each other only occasionally through their connection to Chloe and Donovan. Bryan would soon find another dance partner, another suitable prospect for that wife-and-mother position he was looking to fill. As for Grace…

She tugged at the collar of her linen blouse, feeling it tighten again. She would be fine, she assured herself. She had a life of her own. Maybe she needed to keep that in mind more often, instead of spending so much time lately thinking about…well, other things.

Chloe was still watching her. "I heard you met Bryan's parents last night."

"Where did you hear that?" Had Bryan paid another visit to Chloe while Grace was out of the store for a few minutes earlier?

"Donovan told me. Bryan mentioned to him that his parents made an unexpected appearance at the fund-raiser last night. Donovan asked me if you'd talked about meeting them."

"I guess they slipped my mind."

"What are they like? I never met them, you know."

Grace walked toward their office with Chloe close at her heels. "They seemed pleasant enough, I suppose."

"Donovan hasn't told me much about them, but I

can tell he isn't particularly fond of them. He seems to like Mrs. Falcon better than Mr. Falcon, though.''

''Mr. Falcon did seem a bit more…aloof.'' Except when he had danced with another man's wife, she thought cattily.

''How did Bryan react to them? Did he seem glad to see them?''

''I couldn't say, really. They seem to have a very polite, almost formal relationship. Very different from our bond with our parents.''

''Donovan lost his parents early, you know. He thinks of Bryan as a brother, but he's never considered the Falcons surrogate parents. He's never said so, but I get the impression that they consider him a bit beneath them socially. They seem to treat him more as Bryan's employee than his best friend—or at least that's the impression I've gotten on the rare occasions when he has spoken of them.''

Remembering the way the Falcons had taken pains to spend time with the wealthiest and most influential guests at the fund-raiser, Grace didn't doubt that they were snobs. ''At least he doesn't have to worry about that with our folks. Mom and Dad already think the world of him.''

''And he them. He was a bit overwhelmed at first by the way they welcomed him into the family like a long-lost son, but he's getting used to it. Actually I think he's getting a bit spoiled to Mother's fussing and Dad's attention. I think it's very sweet the way he responds to them. I don't believe even Donovan knew how hungry he was for a family.''

Chloe, of course, was charmed by everything her fiancé did. But Grace had also found it rather touching the way tough, reserved, emotionally awkward Donovan was beginning to respond to her family's demonstrative affection. She couldn't help feeling rather sorry for Bryan, who had grown up the only child of parents who regularly indulged in "discreet dalliances," and who equated monetary gifts with parental affection.

She shook her head slightly, as if to clear it. Had she just found herself feeling sorry for Bryan Falcon? A man who had everything—wealth, looks, intelligence, charm, influence? Maybe he hadn't found a bride who suited him yet, but she had no doubt that was only a matter of time. Bryan could have just about any woman he wanted—with the exception of the Pennington sisters, of course, she added hastily.

He would have little trouble finding someone willing to change herself into anything he wanted in exchange for the privilege of becoming Mrs. Bryan Falcon.

"Is something wrong with your blouse?" Chloe asked. "You keep pulling at the collar."

"I, um, think it must have shrunk the last time it was cleaned. Feels tight."

"It doesn't look too small. Anyway…would you like to join Donovan and me for dinner and a movie tonight? He wants to get away from wedding plans for a few hours. He's picking me up here."

Spending an evening as a third wheel on a date with the lovebirds? "Thanks, but I have other plans for the evening."

"Oh? Are you seeing Bryan tonight?"

"No, he and I have plans for tomorrow—at least, *he* has plans. I'm just going along as a prop."

"Should I remind you again that you can call a halt to this anytime you like?"

"No reminders necessary."

Chloe spent the next few minutes straightening her already-immaculate desk. Grace made a halfhearted, distracted attempt to bring some order to her own. Donovan arrived, and Chloe left with him after Grace offered to lock up and set the security alarms.

Donovan seemed a bit hesitant about leaving her there alone, but she reminded him dryly that she was hardly ever alone these days. She rarely saw Bryan's security people, but she knew they were usually hovering somewhere in the background. She doubted they hung around twenty-four hours a day, but she would bet someone usually made sure she arrived home safely after work. She was growing accustomed to an itchy, nagging feeling of being watched by unseen eyes—but she hadn't learned to like it.

Her plans for the evening did not include a bodyguard.

She made two stops on her roundabout trip home—a video store and the drive-through takeout window of a Chinese restaurant. She wanted to give every indication of a woman who planned to spend her Saturday night alone with egg rolls and Antonio Banderas.

Back at her apartment, she ate the egg rolls, washed them down with a diet cola, then changed from her work clothes into a skimpy, scoop-neck T-shirt and low-riding jeans. A round brush and a curling iron changed her sleek bob into a more rumpled, younger-looking hairstyle, and sultry makeup altered her usual, everyday appearance.

Satisfied that she looked different from the responsible, practical businesswoman who reported to work every day, she slipped out of her apartment. She knew this building very well; there were ways to get out that wouldn't be expected by anyone who'd grown used to her usual routines.

There were times when Grace simply had to escape the imaginary cage she lived in for most of her life.

Chapter Six

The last time Bryan had been this anxious was when Chloe and Donovan were kidnapped a few months earlier. The hours had passed with excruciating slowness during that ordeal when he hadn't known the whereabouts of his friends, or if he would ever see them again. This evening seemed to creep by just as slowly while he paced Grace's apartment, wondering where the hell she had gone.

When he'd phoned Chloe immediately after being notified that Grace was missing, she had downplayed his fears. She had assured him that slipping off for a few hours—or even for a few days—was nothing new for Grace. She had been doing so on an irregular and unpredictable basis since she'd finished college. She didn't even tell Chloe where she went during those absences, only that sometimes she just had to "escape the cage," whatever that meant.

Bryan's concerns had not been assuaged by that information. "You think she deliberately gave my security guy the slip? Even though she's well aware of the reason for the extra precautions at present?"

"I think that's exactly what she did," Chloe had answered, her tone resigned. "I thought she acted a little funny earlier when I asked if she wanted to spend the evening with Donovan and me. She was very evasive about her plans. I should have realized then that she was up to something."

"You have no suggestions of where to look for her?"

"I'm afraid not. Besides, she would be livid if we track her down when she wants to be left alone."

"I'm not really worried about annoying her right now. I'm more concerned about her safety."

"I'm sure she's fine, Bryan. She just needed some time to herself. The past few weeks haven't been easy for her."

She spoke confidently about Grace's safety, but Bryan thought he heard just a hint of anxiety in her voice. Chloe, of all people, knew the risks of being publicly involved with a multimillionaire. The very wealthy always had to be mindful of security, and as long as the mastermind behind the earlier kidnapping was at large, there was added reason for Grace to be careful. The chances were slim that Childers would risk pulling the same criminal stunt a second time, but Bryan considered the possibility just credible enough to warrant extra precautions. Wandering off at night on her own without telling anyone her whereabouts was no way for Grace to cooperate.

"I'm going to wait at her apartment while Jason

and his men look for her,'' he announced abruptly into the phone.

Chloe made no effort to hide the reservation in her voice. "She won't like that."

He was already moving toward his door, his car keys in the hand that wasn't clutching the wireless phone. "Tough. You want me to call you when we find her?"

"Please. No matter what hour it is. Even though I'm sure she's fine."

If Grace really had deliberately shaken the bodyguard he'd assigned to her just to prove she could, she wouldn't be fine by the time Bryan finished with her. She would have several strips of hide missing— at least figuratively.

He just hoped he would have the opportunity to yell at her.

Two hours after completing that phone call, he prowled the few rooms of Grace's apartment, his temper increasing in direct proportion to his concern. It was after 1:00 a.m.; where the hell was she?

More to the point, who was with her?

Needing to do something at least semiproductive, he pushed the send button on his phone, which redialed the last number he'd called only twenty minutes earlier. Jason Colby, head of security for Bryan Falcon Enterprises, answered on the first ring.

"I still haven't found her," Colby said without waiting for his employer to identify himself.

Bryan knew Jason was impatient with this assignment. Bryan had pulled his security chief off another project as soon as he'd been notified that Grace was missing. Jason had suggested that his subordinates could look for Bryan's AWOL faux-girlfriend. Bryan had suggested in return that Jason could look for another job—a threat that was only partially bluff.

Jason had taken over the search for Grace without further protest—as Bryan had known he would.

After being updated on the details of the search, Bryan ordered Jason to keep looking, then disconnected and resumed his pacing. He was tempted to call the local authorities and ask for assistance—an APB on Grace's car, maybe—but he knew that wasn't warranted at this point. Grace had only been gone for a few hours, and there was no evidence that she hadn't simply taken off on her own.

He had an equally strong urge to go out looking for her himself. But his place was here, coordinating the search from behind the scenes. Here, where he would be on hand to greet her if—when—she wandered back in. And that had damned well better be soon, he thought, tossing the phone on the couch in a fit of pique.

He snatched it up again when it rang half an hour earlier. "What?"

"We've found her car," Jason announced.

"Where?"

"She's driving it into her parking space right now."

"Do you know where she's been?"

"No. I just spotted her a couple of blocks from here and followed her back. Want me to escort her up?"

"No. Stay around until she gets into the elevator, then head back to your place for some rest. Send everyone else home, as well. Have the guard back at the usual time in the morning. She won't be going out again tonight."

"Right. I'll talk to you later, then. And, uh, boss—"

"Yeah?"

"Keep that temper of yours under control, okay? You don't want to end up behind bars for disturbing the peace."

"I won't yell," Bryan replied stiffly. He was fully capable of expressing his displeasure without raising his voice.

He heard Grace's key in the lock less than five minutes later. He waited in the center of the room, his feet spread, his arms crossed over his chest, a scowl on his face. Grace had taken only a couple of steps into her apartment, swinging the door closed behind her, when she spotted him.

She gasped loudly and dropped her purse and keys, both of which landed noisily on the hardwood floor at her feet. "*Jeez,* Bryan, you nearly gave me a heart attack. What the hell are you doing in my apartment?"

And then her eyes widened and the color drained from her cheeks. "Has something happened to Chloe?"

"Chloe's fine," he reassured her automatically, even as he took in her appearance. She looked… different. Her hair was tousled, her eyes were emphasized with smoky shadow and liner, and her abbreviated T-shirt clung a bit too faithfully to her breasts. Its hem ended a couple inches above the top of her hip-riding jeans, revealing a well-toned midriff.

She looked great. Which only made his frown deepen. "Chloe is fine," he repeated. "Where the hell have you been?"

Her relief was palpable. "You just took ten years off my life. When I saw you standing there, I thought something must have—"

"You haven't answered my question," he cut in flatly. "Where have you been?"

Her chin rose as her eyes narrowed. "I've been out. And you didn't answer *my* question. What are you doing in my apartment? How did you get in?"

"We can stand here the rest of the night—what little there is left of it, anyway—hurling the same questions at each other, but you might as well know that you aren't getting rid of me until I get some answers. I want to know if you intentionally threw off the security detail I assigned to you—and if so, why."

"I had plans for the evening. If your bodyguard missed seeing me leave, that's not really my problem, is it?"

"It is most definitely your problem if you deliberately slipped away from him. And considering that you must have left the building in a roundabout way that let you get away unnoticed, my bet is that you knew exactly what you were doing."

She bent to pick up her purse and keys, a movement that also allowed her to avoid his eyes. "How long have you been here?"

"Too long." He opened his phone and began to punch in Chloe's number. "I have to call your sister. She's worried sick about you."

Grace looked at him skeptically. "I told Chloe I had plans. The only reason she would be worried is if you got her all upset."

He back teeth ground so tightly together that he could hear his jaw pop. "Chloe understands the reason I've provided security for you, whether you like it or not.''

Donovan answered the call. ''Did you find her?''

''Yeah. She just walked in.'' Bryan watched as Grace tossed her things on a table, then moved into the kitchen to fill a glass with water.

''She's okay?''

''For the moment.''

Donovan chuckled. ''Take it easy on her, Bryan. Chloe told you she was probably fine. But I'll let Chloe know she's home.''

''Do that.'' Bryan disconnected the call, then followed Grace into the kitchen. ''Do you know it's 2:00 a.m.?''

She set her empty glass in the sink. ''I'm perfectly capable of reading a clock. I hope you didn't wake Chloe and Donovan.''

''They weren't asleep. They were pacing the floor with worry about you!'' Damn it, now he was shouting. But she frustrated him to no end with her refusal to answer his questions and her lack of reaction to his temper—or the genuine concern that lay behind the anger.

Once again the look Grace gave him was disbelieving. ''*They* were pacing the floor?''

Because he knew Chloe would mention that she hadn't been overly worried about her sister on this occasion, Bryan growled, ''Well, they should have been. Anything could have happened to you out on the streets by yourself at this hour.''

''I've been living on my own for several years. I'm perfectly capable of taking care of myself.''

''You purposefully eluded the security guard,

didn't you?'' It seemed important to make her admit it.

She shrugged, which he took as an affirmative answer.

''Why?'' he demanded. ''You're free to go anywhere you want and stay as long as you like. The security guard has instructions to remain totally in the background unless you need assistance, so neither you nor anyone else should even be aware of his presence.''

''I'm *always* aware of their presence,'' she snapped back. ''I hate being followed around all the time, knowing that everything I do is being reported straight to you.''

''I don't get reports of everything you do. Hell, Grace, I don't care what stops you make as long as you're safe. The only reports made to me are when the guards go on and off duty, and whether anyone suspicious tried to approach you at any time.''

''Then how did you know to come here tonight? If, as you said, no one saw me leave or knew where I was, how did you know I wasn't in my apartment?''

''The guard noticed your car was missing when he made his final round before leaving for the night. He knew the car was there earlier and it concerned him that he hadn't seen you emerge from the usual exit. He realized the only other way out was the service entrance, which wasn't being watched since it was assumed you were safe in your apartment for the night. He contacted me, as he'd been instructed to do. Because I couldn't believe you would be foolhardy enough to pull a stunt like this, I operated on the assumption that you were in trouble.''

''And you overreacted.''

"Damn it, Grace." He stepped toward her and caught her forearms in his hands. It was all he could do not to shake her. "I was worried about you. You know Wallace Childers is still out there somewhere, and that he still hates me for putting an end to his crooked business practices."

"You told me you were confident Childers has left the country. And that he's too cowardly to come after you or anyone else you care about again."

"I said I was pretty sure that was the case. If I'd been completely confident, I wouldn't have been so insistent about security."

"Well, as you can see, I'm fine. I'm safely home, and I'm sure you'll make certain I don't have a chance to slip out on my own again."

The somberness of her words made him shake his head. "It's only for a little while longer. Just a few more weeks, and this will all be over."

She turned her head away so he couldn't see her expression. "As you pointed out, it's very late, and I'm tired. I'm sorry I worried you, and I'll try not to do so again. I just needed a few hours to myself."

He made a deliberate effort to loosen his grasp on her, though he didn't release her. He wanted to ask her again where she'd been. He bit the words back because he knew he had no right to ask. He would insist on providing her with security, but as long as she cooperated in that respect, she was free to go wherever she wanted. With whomever she wanted.

Instead he said, "If this is getting to be too much for you, we can find a way to end it now. We'll have a public spat or something."

"The deal was, we have our so-called 'break-up' after the wedding so we don't attract any negative attention beforehand. I'm not backing out on my part of the arrangement.''

"But if…''

She broke away from him, her face set in stubborn lines. "I'm sticking with it—unless you want out.''

"No,'' he said quickly. "I still think it's a good plan.''

"Fine. Now go away and let me get some rest.''

"You aren't planning to leave again tonight, are you?''

She rolled her eyes. "It's two in the morning. The only place I'm going is to bed.''

"I don't suppose you want company…''

"Go home, Bryan.''

He managed a weak smile. She assumed, of course, that he'd been joking. This wasn't the time to let her know he'd been quite serious. One sign from her and he'd have her in bed so fast her head would spin. Maybe it was a culmination of his emotions during the past few hours—but he suspected this had been building a lot longer than that. He wasn't sure when, exactly, he'd decided he wanted Grace Pennington, but he had no doubt of it now.

Trouble was, she didn't want *him*. And he didn't know where she had been this evening—or with whom. All in all, his chances with her weren't looking too good at the moment.

Deciding he'd better leave before he dug himself any deeper, he turned toward the door. "Lock the door behind me.''

"Locking the door didn't keep *you* out.''

He only looked at her over his shoulder, waiting until she sighed and joined him at the door. He opened the door, then paused in the doorway. Studying her closely, he saw signs of her weariness—a smudge of purple beneath her eyes, a slight droop to her shoulders. His voice softened when he spoke again, ''I really was worried about you, Grace.''

She moistened her lips with the tip of her tongue before murmuring, ''Um…I appreciate the concern. It just wasn't necessary.''

He would have liked to kiss her then, just to re-assure himself that she was all right. But since he'd spent the past several minutes chewing her out, he doubted that she would be receptive to a kiss from him. He cheered himself with the reminder that he would be spending the next day with her. ''I'll see you tomorrow morning at ten.''

There was little expression on her face when she nodded. ''Good night, Bryan.''

He heard the locks click into place after she closed the door between them. It gave him the depressing feeling that she was locking him out of her life.

Squaring his shoulders, he turned toward the ele-vator, reminding himself that even Grace had ac-knowledged that he wasn't an easy man to lock out.

Even though she was exhausted by the time she crawled into bed, Grace didn't rest well. Her emotions were still in turmoil from her confrontation with Bryan. She was still angry with him for challenging her right to go out without his assigned escort, yet she couldn't help remembering that there had been genuine concern for her in his eyes.

She told herself not to read too much into that. Bryan was the overly responsible type; he'd promised that no harm would come to her because of her as-sociation with him, and he would go overboard in his efforts to keep that promise. He would do the same for anyone.

As for the other overtures he'd been making to her lately—the kisses, the long looks, the unexpected offer to join her in bed, which may or may not have been made in jest—she would have to keep those in perspective, as well. Flirting came as naturally as breathing to Bryan; she'd seen him work that same natural charm on blushing senior citizens.

What really concerned her was the possibility that he was beginning to see her as a substitute for her sister. He'd been attracted to Chloe, and so impressed by her that he'd actually considered marrying her. Was it really so farfetched that he could be transferring those abruptly derailed feelings to Chloe's identical twin?

Bryan had been drawn to Chloe's gentle, peaceful, competent and dependable nature, seeing in her the ideal potential mate for a wealthy, powerful, socially prominent man, and future mother of his children. Except for appearance, Grace was nothing like her sister. Nor was she willing to change to suit anyone's image of what she should be like. Not again.

The best plan of action, therefore, was to continue to demonstrate to Bryan that she wasn't the type of woman he'd been searching for. If he *was* making the mistake of seeing her as a convenient substitute, he had to be shown the error of that thinking. And there was no better way to show him than to be herself around him.

The problem was, she had to keep reminding herself, as well as Bryan, that they were all wrong for each other. There were times when it was a bit too easy to pretend that the charade was real.

The telephone woke her at just after 8:30 a.m. She felt as though she'd only managed a couple hours sleep, and she answered the phone with a yawn. "H'lo?"

"I'm sorry, did I wake you?" Chloe asked.

Grace wriggled to an upright position, pushing her tumbled hair out of her eyes with her free hand. "It's okay. I have to get up, anyway."

"I take it you're uninjured?"

"I'm fine. Sorry Bryan worried you last night with his tantrum."

"Maybe you should have told him you planned to go out last night?"

Grace sighed. "I've already gotten this lecture from Bryan. Don't *you* start."

"He was pretty mad, huh?"

Grace remembered the moment she had first spotted Bryan standing in the center of her living room, his expression forbidding, his posture letting her know he was poised for battle. "You could say that."

"It hasn't been that long since Donovan and I were kidnapped. The nightmare is still fresh to Bryan. I figured you'd just slipped off with some of your friends, but Bryan doesn't know you as well as I do. He was half convinced that Wallace Childers had resurfaced and snatched you for ransom—or revenge."

"He overreacted, obviously. But I'll try not to set him off again."

"You'll cooperate with his security measures?"

"Within reasonable bounds."

"That sounds like another argument waiting to happen—but I'll leave it to you and Bryan to work out between you. You're still seeing him today?"

"He's picking me up at ten."

Chloe cleared her throat. "He was very worried about you last night. It really shook him to think you could be in trouble."

"As I said, he overreacted."

"He seems to be growing quite fond of you. I can tell he's enjoyed the time he's spent with you."

Uh-oh. Grace frowned into the receiver. "Bryan and I have a common interest—making sure you and Donovan have a pleasant, problem-free wedding. That's all there is to it."

"I don't know. I think you're kind of nice together. Bryan thrives on challenges—and you certainly challenge him."

"And I think *you're* getting carried away with your wedding planning. You're seeing everything through a romantic haze."

"Still..."

"Forget it, Chloe. I don't want you playing matchmaker between Bryan and me. You'd be wasting your time."

"Weren't you and Bryan the ones who conspired to bring Donovan and me back together after we were rescued from Childers's men?" Chloe retorted. "The two of you went so far as to strand us together at Mom and Dad's vacation cabin because you decided it was the only way to get Donovan to admit his feelings for me."

"That was different. You and Donovan were obviously in love with each other. You were both too timid and befuddled to do anything about it without a little nudge."

"So maybe *you* need a little nudge?"

"That's the last thing I need," Grace answered flatly. "Bryan and I are nothing more than co-

conspirators. Casual friends with a mutual interest, at most. Promise me you'll stop trying to make any more out of it than that.''

"I just—"

"Chloe." Grace spoke sternly this time, making it very clear the matter wasn't open to discussion. "Promise me."

Sighing heavily, Chloe conceded. "Okay. I'll stay out of it."

"Promise?"

"I promise, okay? Bryan doesn't need my help, anyway. He's not in the least timid about expressing his feelings."

Grace decided to let that statement pass. "I'd better start getting ready. Thanks for calling to check on me."

"Of course. I'll see you later. Call if you want to talk. About anything, okay?"

Grace was well aware that Chloe was always available for her, and she said so before she disconnected the call. Because she was tempted to curl back up in bed and pull the covers over her head, she made herself swing her legs over the side and stand before she changed her mind.

Forty-five minutes later, she had showered, eaten a light breakfast of a bagel and diet cola and dressed in a melon-colored pullover and brief khaki shorts. Bryan had told her to dress casually and comfortably, and she'd taken him at his word.

It was going to be a hot, clear day, the temperature predicted to rise into the upper nineties, and the humidity almost as high. She pulled her hair up into a ponytail, making no effort to restrain the short tendrils that escaped at the back of her neck. She wore minimal makeup and no jewelry other than her functional silver-toned watch. She completed the ensemble with her favorite clunky sandals.

She looked very different from the elegantly dressed and carefully accessorized woman who'd accompanied Bryan to his fancy shindigs during the past few weeks, she decided with a glance at her reflection. This was the real Grace Pennington. No designer labels, no fancy jewelry, no sexy—and excruciatingly painful—high-heeled shoes. If Bryan wanted to be seen with a fashion doll, he could go back to dating his supermodels.

She spent the remainder of her time before he arrived pacing and giving herself a pep talk about how to behave with Bryan today. Not too combative—there was no reason they shouldn't make the best of this outing—but not meekly agreeable to everything he said, either. If he flirted—as he quite likely would—she would respond with nonencouraging stares or chilly half smiles.

She would cheerfully discuss Chloe's wedding, current events or business matters, but she would firmly refuse to talk about last night, making it quite clear that her personal life was none of his concern. They should be able to spend a cordial and pleasant day together for the benefit of whatever tabloid gossips were keeping track of them, and then they would go their own ways again until the next time they decided a public appearance was in order.

It sounded like a good plan—if Bryan would cooperate.

When the doorbell rang, she jumped to her feet, smoothed her hands down her shorts and composed her face into what she hoped was a blandly polite expression. Only then did she open the door. "Good morning, Bryan."

Dressed in a green polo shirt and faded jeans, he was almost hidden behind an enormous bouquet of sunset-orange roses. "Good morning, Grace."

She couldn't help but be impressed by the flowers. They were magnificent, so vividly colored she almost blinked from their brightness. Trust Bryan to choose such an unusual shade rather than the more traditional pink, white or red roses—and to know that this more exuberant color suited her better. "They're beautiful."

"They reminded me of you." He placed the big bouquet in her hands. "Consider them an apology for yelling at you last night. I still disagree with your decision to go off alone the way you did, but I shouldn't have ambushed you about it."

Apparently she wasn't the only one who had vowed to get along today. Studying him over the top of the roses, she noted that his smile didn't quite reach his glittering blue eyes. It was the practiced smile that pushed faint dimples into his lean cheeks and revealed a lot of gleaming white teeth. A smile most people instinctively responded to, even though it revealed absolutely nothing of the thoughts that lay behind it.

She'd always thought of it as the sort of smile a shark would wear when it invited someone to join it for a little swim.

"Thanks. I'll go put these in water." She turned toward the kitchen.

"Nice shorts," he said from behind her.

Now was the time for one of those nonencouraging stares or chilly half smiles. Instead she blushed, stumbled over her own feet and fled to the kitchen.

She seemed to need another quick pep talk.

Her composure reestablished, Grace carried the roses, now arranged in a clear glass vase, back into the living room a few minutes later, setting them prominently in the center of her glass-topped coffee table. "Have you decided yet what we're doing today? I assume you want to go out in public so we'll be seen together."

"Of course. I thought we'd spend the day in Hot Springs, if that sounds okay to you."

"Hot Springs?"

"Where better to be publicly seen than in a town full of tourists?"

She couldn't argue with that. An hour's drive south of Little Rock, the sidewalks of Hot Springs National Park were often crowded with tourists on nice summer weekends. Even dressed in jeans and sneakers rather than one of his expensive tailored business suits, Bryan would draw more than his share of attention. He always did.

It sounded like an innocuous enough day. They would wander cozily among the other tourists, pretending to be two lovers on a Sunday outing, giving Chloe and Donovan privacy to make their plans and enjoy their time together. All in all, it wasn't going to be such a hardship for Grace. Because he seemed to be feeling somewhat remorseful about his middle-of-the-night temper tantrum, Bryan would probably be extra charming today, making sure she had a good time.

All she had to do was play her role—and keep in mind that it was only make-believe.

Chapter Seven

Among his many other talents, Bryan seemed to have a special aptitude for drawing the attention of the media. There should have been nothing particularly newsworthy about a couple spending a summer afternoon strolling the sidewalks of a tourist town. Grace was enjoying the relative anonymity—until they were suddenly thrust once again into the spotlight.

After having a delicious brunch at a local hotel, they wandered through the town on foot for a while. They had just stepped out of one of the many delightful little galleries and were arguing the merits of the featured artist whose works they had just studied in detail. Grace liked them; Bryan thought they were too derivative.

A smattering of other tourists moved slowly around them, pausing to gaze at the eclectic merchandise displayed in shop windows. The high heat and humidity made the air feel a bit thick, as if it required a bit of effort to push through it. Grace was accustomed to Arkansas summer temperatures, of course, but she could spot the tourists who were having a bit more difficulty ignoring the broil-factor.

"So what would you like to do next?" Bryan asked. "A bath house tour? The wax museum? Or we could rent a boat and take it out on Lake Ouachita or..."

"Magic Springs," Grace cut in, because it could take him a while to list all the possibilities available to them.

Bryan's eyebrows rose. "The amusement park?"

She nodded. "I like to eat park junk food and ride the roller coaster."

"In that order?" He chuckled. "Sounds a little risky."

"Only for someone with a weakling's stomach," she scoffed.

"Okay, if you want junk food and thrill rides, then that's what you'll have. Never say I don't..."

The rest of his words were lost in a crash so loud it reverberated through Grace's body. One minute Bryan was standing at her side, and the next he was gone. Spinning toward the street to look for him, she gasped in dismay at the sight of a twisted pile of metal in the four-lane intersection.

It looked as though a big SUV had run a red light and slammed into the passenger side of a smaller car. The smell of gasoline was heavy in the air, along with another, more insidious odor—smoke.

And Bryan was right in the middle of it.

Only vaguely aware of the shouts and cries around

her, Grace ran forward to see if she could help. She had just reached the crumpled car when Bryan thrust a crying child into her arms. "Take him and get back on the sidewalk," Bryan shouted over the pandemonium.

Someone else pushed her out of the way as two strong-looking young men hurried over to assist Bryan. Other spectators hovered in the background, afraid to get close to the mounting heat and smell of fuel.

"It's okay, sweetie. Everything's going to be all right," Grace murmured automatically to the little boy clinging to her neck and sobbing. She guessed that he was about four years old; she had seen Bryan pull him out of the left side of the car. Bryan was now fully inside the car, and she couldn't see him for the smoke and movement surrounding them.

Everyone seemed to be talking at once around her. Snatches of their words drifted toward her.

"It's going to blow up!"

"I called 9-1-1."

"The SUV driver's okay. That's him over there. Hardly looks old enough to drive, does he?"

"Sure hope that car doesn't go up in flames while those people are still in there."

Grace swallowed hard and tightened her hold on the child, maybe seeking comfort as much as offering it. The boy's face was buried in her throat; she could feel wet tears against her skin. "I want my…mama," he whimpered.

Grace patted him again. "Hang in there a minute, kid," she murmured, her attention still focused on that car, from which flames could now be seen quite clearly climbing up the left side from underneath.

The driver was out, being supported by one of the men who had rushed to help Bryan. The woman, whom Grace assumed to be the child's mother, was crying and trying to get back to her burning car. The young man had his hands full restraining her. Someone stepped up to help him. Other people were yelling, some motioning for bystanders to stay back, some running around in seemingly aimless circles. In the distance, the sound of sirens could be heard growing louder as they moved closer.

Grace tried to remind herself that Bryan hadn't been in the car very long. Scant minutes had passed since he'd disappeared inside. It only seemed much longer.

A couple of loud pops were followed by a new spurt of flames from beneath the car. A collective gasp came from the crowd around her, and Grace felt her heart stutter. What was Bryan doing? Why wasn't he coming out?

Her vivid imagination conjured a picture of the car exploding into a fireball with Bryan trapped inside. She flinched from the awful image, telling herself fiercely that it wouldn't happen. Couldn't happen. Bryan wouldn't allow it.

Her knees nearly buckled in relief when he finally emerged from the vehicle. He was immediately pulled away from the car and then surrounded by people. She'd seen that he was holding something, but the bodies between them kept her from seeing what it was. The woman who had been driving the car gave a cry and broke away from the hands that had been holding her back.

A moment later, the car was fully engulfed in flames, despite the efforts of a couple of shop owners who had appeared with fire extinguishers that they were emptying on the vehicles. Bryan would have been in that fire if he'd hesitated even a little longer, Grace realized sickly.

The frantic mother was now holding a tiny bundle in her arms. She turned, searching the crowds around her. "Cody? Cody? Has anyone seen my son?"

The child in Grace's arms responded immediately to the call. "Mama?"

Grace hurried toward the woman. "I have your son. He's fine."

"Thank God." The woman began to cry again.

Bryan put his right hand on the woman's shoulder. "There's a bench beside that shop door. You should sit until the ambulance arrives."

He spoke quietly, but Grace noted that his words carried easily through the babbling of the crowd and the wails of the woman's children. A police car came to a stop in the intersection, and a fire truck wasn't far behind. Settling Cody more securely on her hip, Grace stayed close to his mother while Bryan escorted her and the baby to the bench. The crowd automatically made way for them, of course, after only a glance from Bryan.

What was it about him? Even in jeans and sneakers, his hair all tousled, and his face smudged, he still wore an air of competence and authority that people seemed to instinctively recognize and respond to.

"Aren't you Bryan Falcon?" an older man who had been hovering in the background inquired.

Still focused on the family he'd assisted, Bryan nodded.

"I work at Regions Bank in Little Rock," the man volunteered. "I see you in there sometimes."

Bryan murmured something that was lost in the chaos. Grace heard his name repeated several times around her, and then the police and emergency workers took over. The crowd was efficiently dispersed, the fire was extinguished, and the badly shaken woman and her children were loaded into an ambulance and taken away for observation.

A reporter from the local newspaper arrived, and someone mentioned Bryan's role in the rescue. Grace could hear details being embroidered as she stood there. She was greatly relieved when Bryan had given his statement to the police, answered a few questions from the reporter—downplaying his own part in the rescue, of course—and then turned to Grace to say, "Ready to go?"

"*Yes.*"

The fervency of her reply drew a wry smile from him. "Sorry. I know how you hate being the center of attention."

Aware of all the eyes still focused on them, she cleared her throat and fell into quick step at his side. "Let's just find your car."

Bryan was unusually quiet as they made their way to the parking lot, leaving the noisy gossip and street cleanup behind them. Grace was startled when he turned to her at the car and said, "Would you like to drive?"

"You're offering to let me drive the 'vette?" She frowned at him, studying his face to determine if he was simply making a nice gesture—knowing that she wanted a car like this of her own someday—or if there was something more to the offer. The paleness of his face and the sheen of moisture on his upper lip gave her the answer. "Where are you hurt?"

Looking him over, she saw that he was holding his left arm, which was tucked close to his side; she realized now that he'd kept it there since emerging from the vehicle with the baby girl. "Let me see your arm," she demanded.

He winced when she grabbed his wrist. "Careful."

"Bryan!" She stared in dismay at the outside of his left forearm, which was obviously burned, the skin an angry red with small blisters just becoming visible. "When did this happen?"

"I was having trouble unsnapping the buckles on the baby's car seat. A lick of flame came up the inside of the door, and I shielded her with my arm while I struggled with the buckles."

He said it so matter-of-factly, making it sound like no big deal that he'd used his own arm as a barrier between a spreading fire and a helpless infant. And he hadn't mentioned the injury since, even though his arm had to hurt like hell.

"Why didn't you show this to the paramedics?" she scolded. "These burns need to be treated immediately. Do you *want* to get an infection? It's a wonder you didn't get yourself killed, diving into that car like that."

"I saw the baby in the car seat and I knew the car was starting to burn. Would you have had me leave her in there?"

His calm question didn't soothe her frayed nerves. "Get in the car," she snapped. "I'm taking you to the nearest emergency room."

"Maybe we should drive into Little Rock to get away from the attention here."

"Little Rock is too far. You're just going to have to deal with the attention."

"I really think I..."

"Bryan, get in the damned car!"

He sighed. "Yes, ma'am."

The sheer pleasure of driving Bryan's car was lost in her urgency to find treatment for his arm. She chewed him out almost continuously during the brief drive, and he meekly allowed her to do so. She didn't know if he was being so agreeable because he knew she needed an emotional release from the intensity of the ordeal, or because he was in too much pain to argue with her. Nor was she sure if she was so upset because the whole incident had been so frightening— or because Bryan had been hurt, and could have been killed.

Because it seemed safer to continue lecturing him than to give much thought to her feelings for him, she started in on him again for not immediately reporting his injuries.

"I can't believe that reporter was the first person we saw when we went into the emergency room," Bryan muttered, not for the first time.

"He said he'd driven straight there to check on the condition of the woman and her children. Apparently it was a slow news day." Grace adjusted the rearview mirror of the Corvette and guided the car into the left lane to pass a slower-moving vehicle. Now that Bryan's injuries had been treated and she knew he was going to be all right, she could enjoy the novelty of driving the gleaming silver sports car.

Bryan rested his head against the high back of his black leather seat. "Maybe the story will be confined to the local paper he works for. It probably won't be picked up by the wire services."

"Maybe," she said, but she wasn't particularly optimistic. Bryan's name alone would be enough to propel the story into national news. Add his heroic rescue of a baby to the mix, risking his own life and sustaining injuries in the process, and she could almost guarantee headlines.

He just seemed to have a special talent...

Bryan plucked irritably at the bandages on his left arm. "I don't know why they had to truss me up like this. The doctor even said I wasn't burned that badly."

She could hear the effects of the medications that had been pumped into him; his words were just a bit slurred, his tone uncharacteristically petulant. "The doctor said you were lucky you didn't end up with third-degree burns."

Bryan had been instructed to see his own doctor on Monday, and to take very good care of his burns to keep them from becoming infected. He'd been given painkillers and a list of instructions before being released into Grace's care.

"Sorry about the amusement park," Bryan murmured, his eyes closed. "I know you wanted to ride the roller coaster."

"That's okay."

"Rain check?"

"Sure."

"Good. I'd like to take a wild ride with you."

Because she wasn't sure if that was him or the medicine speaking, she let the comment pass. "I'm just glad no one was seriously hurt in that wreck—including you," she commented. "As violent as the impact was, I was afraid someone had been killed."

"Might have been, if the woman and her kids

hadn't been properly restrained. She was wearing her seat belt and both the kids were buckled into safety seats. They were all bruised and shaken, but not hurt. The SUV's driver—as inattentive as he was to the traffic signals—was at least smart enough to wear his seat belt.''

Bryan still hadn't opened his eyes. He was so still that she might have thought he was sleeping had he not been talking. ''Rest awhile,'' she said. ''I'll let you know when we're home.''

''How can I relax when you're driving my baby? Someone has to make sure you're careful with her.''

She sniffed. ''Go to sleep, Falcon. The meds are making you delirious.''

He chuckled. ''Just be careful.''

A minute later, he was asleep.

Reaching over to make sure his belt was securely fastened, Grace lightly patted his knee. ''Sweet dreams, hot shot,'' she murmured.

She suspected he needed his rest. She would bet that his heroic deeds that day would draw more attention than he expected.

Because she had no intention of leaving Bryan alone on painkillers, Grace drove him to her own apartment so she could keep an eye on him for a few hours. He was still asleep when she parked his car next to her own in the garage. Apparently the medication he'd been given had been quite strong.

''Bryan?'' she said, touching his shoulder. She hoped she could rouse him; she couldn't see herself carrying him to her apartment.

His eyes opened. ''Mmm?''

''Let's go up to my apartment, okay?''

Blinking, he glanced around, taking in their surroundings. "We're at your place?"

"Yes. I'll come around and help you out."

"I can manage." He reached for his door handle, but didn't get very far since he had forgotten to unbuckle his seat belt.

Shaking her head, Grace rounded the front of his car and reached for his door. She decided she'd made a good call bringing him home with her. He was still pretty loopy.

She stayed close when he stood, in case he was dizzy, but he seemed steady enough. He hissed a curse between his teeth when his left arm bumped against the car door, proving the painkillers hadn't taken all the sensation from his wounds.

"Are you okay?"

"I'm fine. It's just sore."

Neither of them said anything else on the way up to her apartment. Grace ushered him inside and closed the door behind them. "Would you like to lie down on my bed?"

"Only if you're offering to lie down beside me."

She gave him one of those chilly smiles she'd been practicing. "Apparently you're still delirious from the medication."

"Maybe…but I'm not an invalid. I don't need to go to bed—not to rest, anyway."

Obviously she had piqued his male ego by being a bit too solicitous. Oh, well, she wasn't very good at that sort of thing, anyway. "How about something to eat, instead?"

He shrugged. "If I can't have you, I suppose I'd settle for a tuna sandwich."

"You're in luck. You picked one of my culinary

specialties.'' She waved him toward the couch. ''Sit. Watch TV or something. I won't be long.''

She heard a baseball game playing on the TV as she moved into the kitchen to make tuna sandwiches. They ate in front of the television. Simple fare, but Bryan seemed to enjoy it. Grace half expected they would root for different teams—it seemed they were always moving in opposite directions—but it turned out they were both Cardinals fans.

Somehow they ended up side by side on the couch, stockinged feet propped on the coffee table, enthusiastically cheering their team. Grace found herself laughing often at Bryan's acerbic comments about the plays that didn't work, the calls he disputed, or some of the more inane remarks from the announcers. If his arm was bothering him too badly, he didn't allow it to show.

It was hard to believe that a day that had taken such dramatic turns could end up so cozily on her couch.

There was a break in the game, and a silly beer ad filled the television screen. Grace glanced at her watch. ''You need to take another painkiller in a few minutes. Can I get you anything else to drink?''

''Thanks, but I still have half a can of soda left.''

''Is your arm hurting?''

He shrugged. ''It's making itself known, but it's tolerable.''

She glanced at his bandages. ''It has to hurt. I've burned myself before and it's awful.''

To illustrate, she twisted her left leg and pointed to a whitish oval scar on the back of her calf. ''I did this on the exhaust pipe of a motorcycle when I was fif-

teen and too dumb to know it was hot. That sucker
hurt like hell for weeks.''

He looked intrigued. ''Were you driving the bike?''

''No, I was riding on the back—barefoot and wearing a pair of shorts. I did have on a helmet.''

''That's encouraging, I suppose. So who was driving?''

''The high school bad boy. Everyone called him
Bodie. His hair was long and his ears were pierced.
He was the first guy I actually knew who had a tattoo.
It was a skull with a snake coming out the mouth.''

''Charming.''

She wrinkled her nose, remembering the thrill of
riding that powerful motorcycle with a boy everyone
considered dangerous. She'd had to sneak around to
see him, since her parents practically went into
spasms every time his name was mentioned.

Bryan eyed her speculatively. ''So far you've mentioned dating a biker and a rodeo cowboy. Drawn to
the rebel type, are you?''

She looked intently at the television screen, where
the baseball game was back in play. ''I suppose I
was—once.''

''What about Chloe? Did she ever tiptoe on the
wild side?''

She gave a short laugh. ''Chloe dated the president
of the chess club. In college, her boyfriend was the
vice president of the College Republicans. Donovan's
the most dangerous man she's ever been involved
with—and he's a white-collar rebel.''

''An interesting way to describe him.''

''A former soldier turned bodyguard turned corporate executive. What would *you* call him?''

''I just call him my friend.''

She took a sip of her soda, then nearly spewed it across the room when she felt Bryan's fingers on her bare leg. She lowered the aluminum can to look at him. "What are you doing?"

"Just looking at your scar—in case mine ends up the same way." He traced the outline of the scar with one fingertip—and it was all she could do not to shiver in reaction.

She tried to speak coherently. "I, uh…maybe you'll luck out and you won't have a scar at all."

"I could always cover it with a tattoo. Would you find that irresistibly attractive?"

She had no intention of admitting that she already came all too close to thinking of him that way. "I told you, I outgrew that sort of thing a long time ago."

He was still stroking her leg—very lightly, his fingertips barely brushing her skin. "What would it take for you to find me irresistible?"

"A miracle," she snapped, shifting her weight on the couch.

He gave her a smile that should have been illegal. "I'm rather good at arranging miracles."

As he spoke, he tickled the back of her knee, a spot she had never realized was particularly erotic—until now. A quiver ran just beneath her skin from that point of contact to the center of her abdomen. She gulped and swung her feet to the floor. "I'll get your pills. I think you need to be medicated again."

"I can wait awhile longer."

But she couldn't. She needed something productive to do before her hormones mutinied against her common sense and caused her to do something really stupid.

She stood and hurried to the kitchen, thinking of how ironic it was that she had brought Bryan to her apartment because she thought he needed someone to take care of him. Turned out that Bryan Falcon was just as hard to handle injured as he was in perfect health.

Chapter Eight

Bryan wouldn't have admitted it to Grace for anything, of course, but his arm hurt like the devil. The burns weren't serious—he'd scorched off the hair and a thin layer of skin—but the abused nerve endings had been punishing him in throbbing waves all afternoon. Especially now that the painkiller had worn off.

The doctor had instructed him to keep the wound clean and dry, and to see his own physician for further care instructions. He had added that the burns were mostly superficial and shouldn't cause any long-term effects. Grace was making too much of the incident, actually, but he couldn't say he disliked being the focus of her solicitude—as endearingly awkward as she was in offering it.

This newest glimpse into her past—her long-ago attraction to the local "bad boy"—intrigued him, as so much about her did. The more time he spent with

Grace, the more he became aware that there were many layers to her, some of them hidden so deeply beneath the surface that it would take persistence and determination for anyone else to uncover them.

Funny. When he'd first met her, he had thought of her as a slightly more acerbic version of Chloe. Now he understood just how erroneous that impression had been.

He admired Chloe a great deal. She was intelligent, witty, kindhearted, competent and serene. A pleasure to be around. She would make his sometimes difficult friend Donovan very happy.

As for her twin—Grace was more complex in some ways than Chloe. Moodier, more reserved, more suspicious—traits that had initially taken him aback, but now made him more interested in learning everything about her. He was curious how a woman so similar to Chloe in appearance, raised at the same time by the same parents, could turn out so differently. It could possibly take years to fully decipher the puzzle that was Grace. Maybe a lifetime.

That errant thought made him clear his throat as she came back into the room carrying a glass of water. Damn, she looked good in those shorts. And now that he knew exactly how silky her long, shapely legs felt, he couldn't wait to get his hands on them again.

She held out one hand to him, revealing two white pills in her palm. "Take these."

"I'll take one of them. You can put the other back in the container."

"You're supposed to take two."

"I don't like that fuzzy-head feeling. And it doesn't hurt that badly, anyway."

"But…"

He settled the issue by plucking one of the pills from her hand and popping it into his mouth. Taking the glass of water, he washed the pill down. "There," he said, lowering the glass. "That should do it."

She shook her head, but didn't try to insist that he take the second pill. After returning it to the container, she stood at the end of the couch, looking as if she wasn't quite sure what to do next. "Would you like me to call one of your people to drive you home?"

"My people?" he repeated, amused by her wording.

"Should I have said one of your minions?"

"Cute. But, no, I don't need one of my 'minions' at the moment. I can drive myself home when I'm ready."

"You aren't supposed to drive or operate heavy equipment while you're taking those pills."

"I'm not planning to use a forklift this evening. I'm just driving home, which is only a few miles from here, I should point out. I would be on the road for all of ten or fifteen minutes."

"That's plenty of time to get into an accident and hurt yourself…or someone else. At least let me call Jason or someone to give you a lift."

"Jason is my security officer, not my chauffeur. He has much more important duties to attend to."

"Then who *is* your chauffeur?"

"I don't have one. I prefer to drive myself."

"Then I'll drive you and call a cab to bring me home."

"Are you so anxious to get rid of me?"

She crossed her arms and looked away from him. "I simply thought you might want to rest. You've had a rather stressful day."

He decided he'd had enough of her benevolence, charming as it was. It was time to point out to her that it would take more than a couple of burns to get the best of him. Rising to his feet, he paused just a moment to let the medication-induced dizziness subside, making sure he gave no sign of the condition. And then he moved toward Grace.

"I haven't found the day particularly stressful. It was very nice, actually. I enjoyed having brunch with you and wandering through the streets of Hot Springs with you. I've had a nice time sitting here watching baseball with you."

"Did you enjoy almost being trapped in a burning car?" she asked cynically. "Having your arm burned? Spending a couple of hours in a hospital emergency room?"

He shrugged. "I'm glad I was able to help that family—though if I hadn't, someone else would have. As for the E.R., I didn't particularly enjoy being swabbed and swaddled, but it was worth even that to spend the day with you."

She rolled her eyes. "There are no microphones hidden in my apartment. You can drop the phony sweet talk."

"Maybe I mean it."

"And maybe you're full of hot air."

He chuckled and reached up to stroke his knuckles along her jaw line. "I really do enjoy being with you, Grace."

Her cheeks darkened. It always fascinated him that she blushed so easily with him. And it pleased him that he could make her do so. The stern frown she gave him didn't quite diminish the effect of the blush. "I'll drive you home now."

"Not just yet. First I want to thank you for taking such good care of me this afternoon."

Her reply was brusque. "You're welcome."

He bent his head closer to hers. "I haven't thanked you yet."

"You don't—"

He smothered whatever she intended to say beneath his lips.

He had kissed her before—to play his part, or to prove a point, or just to shake her up. This time he kissed her for no other reason except that he wanted to. He wanted *her*.

Had she made any effort to push him away, he would have backed off immediately. He gave her every opportunity to do so, holding back at first until he could tell if she was going to respond. At first she froze, holding herself very still for what seemed like forever, and then very gradually, she began to respond. Her lips moved tentatively, experimentally. And when he pulled her closer and deepened the kiss, she parted her lips for him.

The result was powerful enough to almost rock him back on his heels. If Grace kissed this well when she was hardly even trying, he couldn't imagine how it might be when she gave it her all. He couldn't wait to find out.

It seemed there was still a bit of the rebel left in Grace.

He knew he should draw back before the kiss got out of control—as it so easily could. Already his hands itched to caress and explore. The blood was beginning to surge through his veins and pool in his groin. It was only a kiss, but it could so easily develop into more.

He found the resolve to pull away by reminding himself that Grace would probably bolt if he tried to move too quickly. He would have to start all over winning her trust—what little he had gained thus far.

He half expected Grace to turn away when he ended the kiss—to either pretend it hadn't happened or to bluster and blame him for initiating it in the first place. He'd figured out that bravado was her way of hiding insecurities she didn't want anyone else to see.

Instead her gaze held his as she smoothed her hands down the sides of her shorts and cleared her throat. "Well," she said after a moment. "I suppose that was an emotional release, of sorts. It was a more traumatic day than you've admitted, wasn't it?"

So she had decided to be calm and analytical about the kiss. He would almost prefer one of her fiery flashes of temper. At least that would indicate that he wasn't the only one who'd been affected on an emotional level. "That's what you think we were doing? Letting off steam?"

She did turn away then, her expression half-hidden from him. "Of course. What else?"

What else? He didn't think she was ready to hear his theories about that yet. "Maybe I'd better go now," he said instead.

She turned back to face him. "I'll drive you."

"If you insist. You can bring the car back here. I'll have it picked up tomorrow."

Her eyebrows rose. "You would let me keep it overnight?"

"Of course. If anything happens to it, I'll simply take it out of your hide."

That made her smile, as he had hoped it would. As much as he liked his car, it wasn't quite as important to him as Grace implied. He could buy a fleet of sports cars if he wanted. But he enjoyed watching Grace's pleasure with the vehicle—not that he was stupid enough to offer again to buy her one.

There was no more talk about the kiss during the drive to the house he maintained in a gated neighborhood on the Arkansas River. In fact, there was very little talk at all. Bryan leaned back against his seat, trying not to be too obvious about watching Grace as she drove. And while they might not have talked about the kiss, that didn't mean he stopped thinking about it, replaying it in his mind, wondering what might have happened if he'd taken the risk of carrying it further.

He'd kissed Chloe a couple of times during their few dates. They had been friendly kisses at the end of the evenings. Warm and affectionate, but hardly passionate. At the time, he'd considered himself holding back until Chloe had a chance to decide what she wanted from their relationship. Only now did he realize that he'd subconsciously sensed that they weren't right for each other, no matter how diligently he had tried to convince himself that they were.

It had been easier with Chloe, in some ways. He'd known exactly where they stood and what he had thought he wanted from her. He had liked her, admired her, respected her. She'd met almost every qualification he'd listed for a potential mate.

When she'd been kidnapped, he had been frantic with worry about her, and guiltily furious that her association with him had put her in danger. But even then, Grace had occupied his thoughts almost as much as Chloe. He'd spent those days reassuring her that he would bring her sister safely back to her, and dealing with her fear and anger. He'd sat quietly while Grace had released her roiling emotions by yelling at him, and he had watched over her when stress and exhaustion had finally caught up with her and she'd fallen asleep on his couch.

His resigned acceptance when Chloe told him there would be no future for them had proved his heart had never been involved in their experimental courtship. The quiet pleasure he'd felt when he'd realized that Chloe and Donovan had fallen in love demonstrated once and for all that he'd never thought of Chloe as more than a good friend.

His feelings about Grace weren't nearly as clear-cut. Nor was he at all confident about how to proceed from here with her.

Grace was always uncomfortable in Bryan's house. Though there was nothing she would describe as ostentatious about the place, she saw signs of his wealth everywhere she looked. The strict security measures established by the community. The marble and crystal and fresh flowers in his foyer. The awareness that he could have almost anything he wanted at the touch of a button. And, even more incredible to her, the knowledge that this wasn't his only home. He maintained apartments in at least two major cities—that she knew of, at least.

"Is there someone here to take care of you if you need anything?" she asked, moving around the quiet entryway. "A housekeeper or bodyguard or valet, maybe?"

"My housekeeper doesn't sleep over. I don't employ bodyguards for myself, and I've never in my life had a valet," he replied, his expression a mixture of amusement and exasperation. "I'm perfectly capable of taking care of myself, Grace."

Feeling a bit foolish—what did she know about how the very rich lived?—she shrugged and handed him the plastic container of pills he'd been given at the hospital. "Take these when you need them. They'll help you rest tonight. And don't forget to see your doctor tomorrow, just to make sure there are no complications."

"I'll remember."

"Do you want me to take your car to work in the morning? You can have someone pick it up there and I'll hitch a ride home with Chloe."

"That will be fine."

She nodded. "Then if there's nothing else you need, I'll be on my way."

"Are you going straight home?"

She gave him a look. "Don't worry. I'm not going joyriding in your car."

"That isn't what concerns me, and you know it."

She sighed. "Yes, I'm going straight home. I plan to spend the rest of the evening doing laundry and watching mindless TV programs, okay? I'll lock myself in and I won't open the door to strangers. You can give your security guy the night off."

He looked at her for a moment as if he were trying to decide whether he could believe her—which only annoyed her more, of course—and then he nodded. "I'll call you tomorrow."

"Fine." She turned toward the door.

His hand was on the knob before she could reach for it. "Grace?"

Instinctively she tensed, anxious about what he might say now. "What?"

"It was more than blowing off steam."

She didn't have to ask him to clarify the quietly spoken remark. He was referring to the kiss she had been trying very hard not to think about. Nor did she intend to ask him why he had kissed her, if not as an emotional release. When it came to Bryan Falcon, she had decided that her new motto should be, "Better safe than sorry."

Because she couldn't think of anything at all to say, she kept her mouth shut, simply gazing at him until he smiled ruefully and opened the door for her. "Drive carefully."

She nodded and stepped through the door, saying over her shoulder, "G'night, Bryan. Take care of your arm."

She almost ran to the car. She couldn't help glancing into the rearview mirror several times on her way home to make sure Bryan wasn't having her followed—for her own good, of course.

He was becoming entirely too embroiled in her life. If she wasn't very careful, he could invade parts of it that she had fiercely protected for years.

The rescue made the headlines, of course. Grace heard about it the minute she walked into the shop Monday morning.

"I know Bryan's making sure you and he are in the public eye, but does he have to be quite so dramatic about it?" Chloe asked, looking up from the newspaper spread on the counter in front of her.

"Very funny."

"Donovan almost went nuts this morning when he heard about this. He had to leave immediately to make sure Bryan was okay. He's probably still chewing him out for playing the hero and getting himself hurt.''

"I already gave him that lecture. He scared the bejeebers out of me. But, really, Chloe, what else could he have done? He pulled a little boy out of the car and then he went back in for the baby. If I'd been the one who'd gotten there first, I'd have done the same thing. Who wouldn't try to save a helpless baby?''

"A lot of people wouldn't—not if it meant risking their own lives.''

"Bryan never even hesitated. I don't think he gave a thought to his own safety.''

"He wouldn't.'' Chloe smiled and folded the paper. "He wasn't 'acting the hero.' He was simply being himself.''

"Let's not get carried away with his praises.'' Grace walked into the office to stow her purse and place the keys to Bryan's car in her desk drawer. She assumed someone would be along soon to collect it.

Chloe followed her into the room. "How is Bryan, really? He told Donovan on the phone that the burns were only superficial, but the newspaper accounts made them seem much worse.''

"I think you could say the truth lies somewhere between those two reports.''

"Did his arm look very bad?''

Remembering Bryan's raw, red skin, Grace nodded. "I've seen worse, but yeah, it looked painful.''

"You know, Justin and I can handle things around here today if you think you should spend some time with Bryan.''

Grace looked at her sister blankly. "Why would I do that?''

"You know—to take care of him."

"You've got to be kidding."

Chloe made a face. "Honestly, Grace, he's been hurt. He was burned saving lives. It just seems like it would be a nice gesture if you spent some time with him today."

"He has plenty of people to take care of him. You said yourself that Donovan rushed to his side this morning. Heaven only knows how many others did so."

"I just thought you…"

"Don't *you* start believing the stories, Chloe. None of this is real."

Chloe frowned. "His injuries are real. Even for the sake of the charade, don't you think it looks odd that you aren't with him today?"

"I don't think anyone's paying that close attention to us," Grace returned. "Besides, he really wasn't hurt that badly. It was hardly worse than a very bad sunburn. Painful, but not exactly life-threatening."

Chloe looked dissatisfied. "It's your decision, of course."

Grace saw no need to admit that she had tossed and turned for most of the night reliving those long minutes when Bryan had been in the car and the smell of gasoline and smoke had been heavy in the air. She wouldn't admit that his burned arm had been the first image in her mind when the alarm had awakened her from a fitful sleep. Confessions like that would only encourage the disquieting matchmaking urge Grace had seen in her sister lately.

She glanced at her watch. "We'd better get to work. It's almost time to open."

She thought she did a fair job of hiding her distraction as she worked. Only a few times did someone have to say her name repeatedly to get her attention. She only stocked items on the wrong shelves twice, and incorrectly answered only a few customer questions. More than once she found herself standing beside the phone, one hand on the receiver, even though there wasn't anyone in particular that she needed to call.

She worked through her lunch break, explaining that she wasn't hungry when Justin offered to make a food run. Finally, at just after 2:00 p.m., she went into her office, picked up the phone and dialed Bryan's mobile phone number. It was the number he'd given her to use whenever she needed to talk to him; he kept that phone with him at all times, answered it himself, and gave the number out only to a very few.

He answered on the second ring. "Hello?"

"Bryan, it's Grace."

His voice changed instantly from brusque and businesslike to warm and intimate. "Good afternoon, Grace. How are you today?"

She wished she knew what it was about him that even the sound of his voice made a shiver run through her. Sometimes she felt like a silly schoolgirl around him, foolishly impressed by his looks and his charm and his big-man-on-campus walk. "I'm the one who should be asking that question. How are *you?* Did you see your doctor?"

"First thing this morning. Donovan accompanied me to the clinic."

Grace laughed. "From your tone, I would guess that Donovan dragged you to the doctor's office."

"That's another way of phrasing it. But either way,

I'm fine. My doctor assures me I'll heal completely. Probably won't even scar permanently, except for maybe a couple of small spots."

"So I guess you won't need that tattoo, after all."

"Only if you want me to get one."

She wrinkled her nose, even though he couldn't see the face she made. "I think we've covered this territory already."

"Right. Just let me know if you change your mind. I was thinking of something along the lines of a skull with a rose between its teeth."

She remembered the word he'd used when she'd described Bodie's tattoo. "Charming."

"It could even have your name printed beneath it."

"Gee, thanks, but no, thanks. Anyway, the reason I called…"

"You mean it wasn't just to hear my voice?"

"The reason I called," she repeated firmly, "was to ask about your car. No one's come by to collect it yet."

"There's no rush. My doctor doesn't want me to drive for another few days, anyway, because of the meds I'm taking. And I have the Navigator if I need a vehicle for any reason."

He probably had access to half a dozen vehicles, she thought wryly. Which didn't answer her question. "So what should I do about the Corvette?"

"Drive it," he replied. "Keep it a week or so and see if you like having one as much as you thought you would—just for future reference, of course."

She frowned, torn between the temptation of having his car at her disposal for a few days and suspicion of his motives for offering it. "What if something happens to it?"

"The car's insured. Just make sure you don't hurt yourself. Drive carefully and wear your seat belt. Oh, and don't touch the exhaust pipe. It gets hot."

"Very funny," she muttered as he chuckled at his own witticism.

"Really, Grace, I don't need the car right now and you enjoy driving it. So why not? I'll take it back as soon as my arm's better."

She wasn't made of stone. "Okay. Thanks. I'll be careful with it."

"I know you will. So how about picking me up for dinner tomorrow night? I'd ask you for tonight, but to tell the truth, my arm's throbbing like crazy after the doctor messed with it today, so I think I'm just going to crash at my place and catch up on some paperwork."

"Um—dinner? Tomorrow night?"

"Yes. I'd like to go someplace public to show everyone I'm up and about. I've heard there are rumors going around that I practically toasted myself yesterday. That sort of gossip is bad for business."

It made sense. She, of all people, knew how quickly rumors could get out of hand. "Okay, but let's not make it anyplace fancy. I'm not in the mood for snooty."

He chuckled again. "We'll pick someplace busy and casual. Lots of visibility, plenty of background noise to cover our conversation. We could even have Chloe and Donovan join us and make it a party. How does that sound?"

Very safe. She didn't quite trust herself to be alone with Bryan at the moment. Not with the memory of his kisses so clear in her mind. "Perfect."

"So you'll pick me up around seven?"

"Fine."

"Great. I'll make arrangements with Donovan."

"See you tomorrow, Bryan."

"I'll be counting the moments, darling."

She hung up on him. And then she couldn't help laughing ruefully at the sheer brass of the man.

Chapter Nine

To fulfill Grace's request to keep the outing public and casual, the foursome chose a popular Italian chain restaurant in west Little Rock for dinner. The place wasn't as crowded on this Tuesday evening as it was on weekends, of course, but most of the tables were still full.

Grace noted that several of the other diners recognized Bryan, some greeting him by name. Little Rock was a relatively small community and the Falcons had been a familiar part of local society for years. Wearing a lightweight long-sleeve shirt to hide his bandages, Bryan moved through the restaurant with his usual brisk confidence, showing no sign of weakness from his adventures Sunday afternoon.

Chloe and Donovan were waiting at a table when Grace and Bryan finally made their way across the room. Donovan glanced up from the menu he'd been studying. "Well, if it isn't 'millionaire investor Bryan Falcon and his frequent companion.'"

"Very funny," Grace said, sliding into the chair Bryan held for her.

"Isn't it strange that every article phrases that exactly the same way?" Chloe mused. "Is there, like, an official stylebook that tells reporters how to refer to well-known people?"

Bryan shrugged as he took his own seat. "It just becomes habit. Once someone has been 'labeled' by a reporter, the others repeat the label by rote."

"Just as Donovan is always referred to as Bryan's 'close friend and business associate,'" Grace pointed out, repaying Donovan for that "frequent companion" reminder.

Donovan nodded. "Better than some things they could call me, I guess. I'm hungry. Anyone have a recommendation for a good dish here?"

They spent the next few minutes discussing the menu, then placed their orders. While they waited for their food to be served, they carried on the conversation over glasses of wine and slices of herbed bread dipped in olive oil and pepper.

Grace noted that Bryan quickly changed the subject whenever his injuries or the rescue during which he'd incurred them were mentioned. It was obvious that he wanted to put the incident behind him. He was certainly not one to bask in his own heroics. He successfully diverted the conversation by asking Chloe how the wedding plans were coming along. Chloe happily obliged.

They were well into their meal when someone suddenly slapped Bryan on the back, hard enough to nearly knock him from his chair. Because they'd been so involved in their food and conversation, none of them had noticed the man's approach until he struck Bryan. Donovan started to rise, his expression dark, his body poised for trouble, but Bryan motioned him back into his seat after a glance over his shoulder.

"Hello, Peter," he said, and Grace detected little pleasure in his voice.

"Falcon. Hope I didn't hurt you just now. I forgot you got yourself injured over the weekend."

Yeah, right, Grace thought. She disliked the man on sight. Pompous and phony were the first words that jumped into her mind when she looked at him, with his designer emblazoned clothes, his flashy gold jewelry and his fluffed-and-sprayed hairpiece. He looked familiar, she thought, narrowing her eyes thoughtfully at him and wondering if she had met him before.

"Everyone, this is Peter McMillan," Bryan said for etiquette's sake. "Peter's a local attorney I've had some dealings with over the years. Peter, these are my friends Grace Pennington, her sister, Chloe, and Donovan Chance."

Grace knew who the guy was now. His tacky get-fast-money-for-every-imagined-injury television ads ran frequently on local cable channels. They were so annoying that she always pressed the mute button on her remote control when they came on.

Too bad she didn't have such a button now.

McMillan looked from Grace to Chloe and back again. "Now, let's see," he said. "You were dating this one—" he pointed to Chloe "—and then you switched to this one, right?" His stubby finger stabbed in Grace's direction.

He was talking to Bryan, of course, but everyone

at the table stiffened. Donovan started to rise again; Chloe rested her hand quickly on his arm. He subsided with a low growl and a glare for McMillan.

"Been reading the tabloids, Pete?" Bryan asked quietly.

After glancing rather warily at Donovan, the other man shrugged. "That's where I find most of my clientele."

"Doesn't surprise me. But as it happens, Grace and I have been seeing each other for some time. You've made the same careless mistake others have made— mixing up the twins."

"Did I?" McMillan didn't look convinced, but since there was no way he could prove differently, he settled for a cap-toothed smile. "That's not hard to do when they're so identically lovely."

If he'd hoped to please anyone, he failed. Only stony silence greeted the compliment.

He cleared his throat. "Well, I'll be seeing you around the courthouse, Falcon. Enjoy your dinner."

Bryan nodded and turned back to his food, apparently putting the other man completely out of his mind.

"I don't know how you could be civil to that slime," Donovan muttered, his own appetite seemingly ruined. "I wanted to punch his smarmy face in."

"And that would have landed all of us right in the headlines of the gossip rags again. And you in jail," Chloe reminded her temperamental fiancé. "Bryan handled the guy exactly right, cordially sticking with the stock response we've all been using for the past few weeks."

"That rodent is a friend of yours?" Grace asked Bryan in disbelief.

"Hardly. I've crossed paths with him a few times when his clients tried frivolous lawsuits against some of my business holdings. He's never won, but I doubt that he's given up. It galls him that I have money he can't seem to get his hands on."

"I'm with Donovan," Grace said. "I'd be tempted to punch his teeth out."

Bryan smiled at Chloe. "Bloodthirsty pair we're involved with, aren't they?"

Chloe laughed and agreed. Grace turned her frown toward Bryan. She started to remind him that he and she weren't involved, especially not in the same way Chloe and Donovan were, but the server appeared just then to ask if they would like dessert. The guys ordered sweets; Grace and Chloe both passed.

"I have to fit into a wedding gown in less than three weeks," Chloe said with a smile.

"And I'll be wearing a snug-fitting bridesmaid's dress," Grace agreed.

Bryan mugged for Donovan. "You don't think this piece of cheesecake will make me look fat in my best-man tux, do you?"

"I don't know." Donovan twisted in his chair to look over his shoulder. "I just hope my dessert doesn't go straight to my butt."

Because it was so rare for Donovan to be silly, and especially so soon after he'd been glaring in anger, the others all burst into laughter. Several heads turned at nearby tables to look at them, and Grace was wistfully aware that they must look like two very happy couples. It was unlikely that anyone could tell only one of the pairings was real, or that she and Bryan would go separate directions soon.

The thought made her amusement fade, though she made an effort to hold on to her smile—for the sake of the other diners and her companions.

They separated a short while later in the parking lot outside the restaurant. Donovan and Chloe left in his car, leaving Grace to drive Bryan home in the Corvette. She had planned to drop him off at his door and drive away without going inside the house herself. She should have known better than to make any plans where Bryan was concerned.

"Come on, Grace, just for a minute," Bryan said as they sat in the car in his driveway. "I would really like you to see the painting I told you about."

She sighed and turned off the car engine. "All right. But only for a little while. I have some things to do this evening."

"Of course. It's just that we can't discuss the painting unless you've seen it first."

That was true, of course. One of the things she and Bryan had in common was a pleasure in art, and they frequently discussed the work of various artists. More often than not they even agreed on what they liked, though when their tastes differed, it was radically. She supposed there was little harm in looking at the painting he wanted her to see, as long as she was careful.

She'd been inside Bryan's house only two or three times, and had never gone beyond the front rooms. She glanced covertly around as he led her down an art-lined hallway toward the back of the exquisitely decorated house. Each framed work was lit with cleverly placed spotlights, making her feel almost as if she were walking through a museum. Yet there wasn't a cold or institutional feel to the place; she could rather easily picture herself decorating in just this way—if she had the money, of course.

He led her into a room that made her catch her breath in a wave of sheer envy. She thought of it as a combination library and gallery, with ceiling-high shelves of books interspersed with paintings and sculptures. A cursory glance at the book titles revealed an eclectic mix of titles, just as the artworks represented several artistic styles and disciplines. "This room is fabulous," she breathed.

"Thanks. I spend a lot of time in here."

She glanced at the deep leather chairs scattered comfortably around the room, each accompanied by a reading light. "I imagine you do."

He crossed the room and motioned to a painting above an antique mahogany library table. "This is the painting I told you about."

Done in the impressionistic style, the painting depicted the historic Old Mill in nearby North Little Rock, an architecturally significant site that had been shown in the opening scene of the movie *Gone With the Wind*. The grays and browns of the concrete used to make the mill blended into the blues and greens of the surrounding water and trees. A touch of color in the background hinted at the onset of fall, as if the scene were poised at the brink of changing seasons. The sun seemed to be setting; long shadows deepened the corners of the canvas. "This is wonderful. You said it was painted by a teenager?"

"The son of one of my employees. I was his first paying client."

"But you won't be his last," Grace predicted,

imagining the generous sum Bryan must have offered for the painting. "He's very talented."

"He'll be even better when he finds his own voice. He's still experimenting with styles. But I have no doubt he'll be an important member of the art world in a few years."

Grace found her attention turning from the painting to the man who owned it. Bryan was a study in contrasts. This room was a prime example—mysteries and thrillers spine-to-spine with works on philosophy and economics, master paintings and sculptures displayed alongside the work of an ambitious teenager. It reminded her of the many roles she had seen Bryan play—shrewd businessman, charming suitor, smooth operator on the social scene. She thought of his slick handling of the press, his cool rebuff of the obnoxious lawyer at the restaurant, the warmth of his relationships with his friends, and the dangerous look in his eyes when he had confronted the man who'd arranged Chloe's kidnapping.

He fascinated her. Entirely too much. She pushed her hand through her hair and turned toward the doorway. "Thank you for showing me the painting. I guess I'd better be going now."

He caught her arm. "What's your hurry? Wouldn't you like to stay and have a cup of coffee?"

"No, really. I need to…"

What? She was sure there was something pressing she should do, but nothing was coming to her at the moment. The closer Bryan leaned toward her, it seemed the blanker her mind became.

How did he do that to her?

"The truth is," Bryan murmured, reaching up to

touch her cheek, "I'm reluctant to see you leave. As I've said before, I enjoy being with you, Grace."

She swallowed and told herself to look away from him, but his glittering blue eyes held hers captive. "Bryan—"

"Grace," he said, and lowered his head just a couple inches more, so that his mouth rested lightly on hers.

Her lips brushed his when she tried to speak. "I really should…"

"Stay a little longer? Definitely."

She shook her head slightly—which turned out to be a mistake since it only increased the pressure of his lips against hers. "I don't…"

"Want to leave? Then stay." He ran his hands down her arms, drawing her nearer.

Her mind seemed to be swirling, her thoughts getting all jumbled and confused. "This really isn't…"

"A time to talk? I absolutely agree," he said in satisfaction.

He pressed his mouth firmly against hers before she could stammer out any more unfinished inanities.

She could have resisted, of course. She could have pushed him away or turned her head or bolted from the room. All those possibilities, along with a few dozen more, flitted through her mind, but she didn't act on any of them. Instead she just stood there, her eyes closed and her hands dangling uselessly at her sides.

He kissed her gently at first, his mouth warm and persuasive against hers. It occurred to her that tilting her head just a little to the right would give him better access. She discovered a moment later that she'd been right; this angle was definitely better.

He wrapped his good arm around her and increased the pressure of the kiss until her lips parted instinctively. She should have anticipated that Bryan would take immediate advantage of that slight concession. He deepened the kiss, a bit tentatively at first, and then more boldly when he met with no resistance.

Grace raised her hands to his chest, clutching his shirt. It wasn't that she was trying to hold him there, she assured herself hazily. It was just that she needed the support; she was suddenly feeling a little dizzy.

Even as she allowed herself to linger in the embrace—even to participate in it—a distant part of her mind searched for rationalizations. She wasn't sure she could get away with the emotional release excuse again—there hadn't been any great crises to pump them up today. And she certainly couldn't claim that Bryan hadn't given her a chance to turn away; he'd certainly initiated the kiss, but he hadn't forced it. She could have stopped it at any time, and they both knew it.

She hadn't wanted to stop it.

As it happened, it was Bryan who finally lifted his head. He wasn't smiling when he searched her face. He looked as though he was trying to decide what to say, which she found surprising because words always came so easily to Bryan.

She bit her lower lip, at a loss for words herself. It was getting harder to blithely ignore their kisses, harder to deny the fact that there was an attraction between them that only seemed to grow stronger as they spent more time together. What she didn't know was whether that attraction was merely physical, at least on Bryan's part. If so, her identical appearance to her sister was definitely a troublesome factor in the equation.

She made herself release his shirt and step back, shoving her hands into the pockets of her slacks. "I'd better go," she said, wondering why he was suddenly being so quiet.

"It is getting late," he agreed, which surprised her all over again because she had expected him to urge her to stay a little longer.

She told herself she wasn't disappointed that he hadn't—and knew that she was lying.

Bryan had already turned toward the door. "I'll walk you out."

Hadn't she just observed to herself that he was a man of contradictions? She studied his back as she followed him down the long hallway, wondering why he had suddenly turned distant and unreadable. What thought had entered his mind to convince him that they should draw back before things got out of hand between them? It depressed her to wonder if he had been thinking of Chloe at the same time Grace had.

"You'll drive carefully on your way home?" he asked at the door.

"Of course. Don't worry about your car."

"You know I'm not concerned about the car."

"I'll be careful," she repeated.

"I'll see you tomorrow, then. We need to talk soon."

At that moment, she didn't even want to know what he thought they should talk about. Right then, she just wanted to escape.

She needed to have a long, stern talk with herself.

Something had changed. Bryan wasn't sure when it had happened, but suddenly he found himself thinking of Grace Pennington in an all-new way. He'd already been aware of his physical attraction to her, but he had tried to convince himself it was a passing fancy.

The attraction wasn't passing. Just the opposite, in fact.

After he and Chloe had parted ways, he had decided to reevaluate his plan to marry and start a family within the next year. He'd convinced himself that if it hadn't worked out with Chloe—the ideal candidate, according to his list of qualifications—then it probably wasn't meant to be at all. Maybe he just wasn't cut out to be a family man. He should be content with his success in business.

It wasn't as if he didn't have female companionship when he wanted it. He just couldn't see himself spending the rest of his life with any of the women he had dated in the past—not even the one he had proposed to before Chloe. The lovely starlet had seemed so crazy about him—until he'd pulled out the prenuptial agreement his lawyers had prepared. She'd certainly shown her true colors then, making it very clear that she had been more intent on winning his fortune than his heart.

Hadn't he humiliated himself enough when it came to his awkward attempts at serious courtship?

When he'd first met Grace, he would have said he couldn't imagine spending the rest of his life with her, either. Now…

Now he needed to do a great deal of thinking about what he really wanted with Grace Pennington.

Grace drove her own car to work on Wednesday. In a funny sort of way, Bryan's car had begun to represent the man, himself. Sexy, powerful, expensive, flashy. And addictive. It wasn't easy going back to her ordinary, functional economy car after driving Bryan's Corvette for a few days. And it wasn't hard to extend that analogy to her collaboration with Bryan, himself.

She was getting much too accustomed to having him in her life. To seeing him frequently, hearing his voice on the telephone. Having him touch her. Kiss her. It wouldn't be easy to go back to her former life without him in it. A life that had been frequently stifling and vaguely unsatisfying before. She didn't even want to think what it would be like to return to those predictable routines now.

She had been at work for only an hour or so when her mother called. Chloe had made a bank run, so Grace left Justin in charge of the shop while she took the call in her office. "Hi, Mom."

"Good morning, honey," Evelyn Pennington, a native of Birmingham, Alabama, replied in her slow, soft drawl. "How's the business going?"

"Great. We're putting Bob on full-time starting next week, and we're hiring another part-time clerk."

"That sounds good. Maybe with more help, you and Chloe can have a little more free time."

"Maybe. Chloe's going to want to spend time with Donovan, of course, and she'll need the freedom to travel with him when he has to go out of town. Justin and Bob and I will be able to run things when she's gone, especially if we hire someone else for a few hours a week. We interviewed a woman yesterday who's looking for ten to twenty hours work a week, just to give her something to do while her kids are in

school. Chloe and I both liked her, so we'll probably
give her a call later today and offer her the job.''

''Be sure you manage some free time for yourself,'' her mother warned. ''Chloe doesn't expect you
to take on too much responsibility just because she'll
be a newlywed. You have a life of your own to live.''

Really, Mom? And what life is that? The cynical
question flashed through Grace's mind, but she kept
it to herself, merely replying, ''I know. I won't
overdo it.''

''See that you don't.''

Grace smoothly changed the subject. ''How's everything there?''

Grace's parents lived in Searcy, a medium-sized
town an hour north of Little Rock. ''Your daddy's
arthritis is acting up some, but everything else is fine
here. Everyone's getting ready for the big party.''

Secure in the privacy of her office, Grace made a
face. Since Chloe and Donovan had decided to be
married at the church Chloe attended in Little Rock,
some of her mother's long-time friends had decided
to hold a prewedding party in Searcy this weekend.
It would be a big event, to be held at the country club
their golf-obsessed father had joined years ago. It
would be much more casual than the events Bryan
attended so often, but Grace wasn't looking forward
to this gala any more than she had the others.

She would know most of the people at this event,
unlike the ones she had attended with Bryan, at which
nearly all the other guests were strangers to her. That
wasn't necessarily a good thing. People who had
known her since she was in diapers showed no hesitation to comment on her personal life. She expected
to field a lot of nosy questions about her relationship

and her future with Bryan—who, of course, would be accompanying her.

She predicted that several would point out that her thirtieth birthday was only a few months away, and that she didn't want to wait too long to start a family. She would hear plenty of broad hints that she and Bryan should quickly follow Chloe and Donovan's matrimonial example.

She hadn't minded so much deceiving the press or the other society gossips. But she was not looking forward to lying to the people she'd grown up among, talking about a future that wasn't going to happen. She wasn't sure her acting skills were good enough to convince her old friends that she and Bryan were in love, and had been involved for some time.

Her parents knew the truth, of course. Donovan had insisted on telling them everything when he and Chloe announced their engagement. Chloe had been very closemouthed about her discussions with Bryan before she met Donovan, and her parents weren't pleased to hear that she'd been considering a marriage that would have been little more than a convenient, businesslike arrangement.

They had reminded Chloe that they had raised her to understand the purpose and the sanctity of marriage. Just because a man and a woman liked each other and shared a mutual desire for children didn't mean they should take marriage vows together. It was their mother who had added that a ticking biological clock was no substitute for a rapidly beating heart. Chloe had groaned in response to that overly fanciful analogy—as had Grace—but Chloe had finally convinced their parents that she had come to her senses.

She and Donovan were marrying for all the right reasons.

Like Grace, their parents weren't happy about the elaborate charade Bryan had concocted to divert gossip from his and Chloe's former relationship, but they had understood the reasons behind the scheme. They had seen how bothered Donovan had been by rumors that he had disloyally pursued a woman who was already involved with his best friend. No one else could have known how hard Donovan had resisted his feelings for Chloe for that very reason.

Evelyn and Hank Pennington had understood that embarrassment and concern for Donovan's feelings had dimmed some of Chloe's sheer joy in her engagement. They had reluctantly conceded that Bryan's plan was worthwhile if it would draw media attention away from Chloe and Donovan—and if Grace didn't mind being the subject of public scrutiny, herself. They had known even as they spoke that Grace would do almost anything for her sister.

"Grace?" her mother prodded, reminding her that it was her turn to speak. "Are you still there?"

"Oh. Yeah, sorry, Mom. I got distracted for a minute. You said something about the party?"

"Yes. Everything seems to be on track, from what the hostesses have told. They're really going all out. Not that it will be anything like those fancy shindigs you and Bryan have been attending, of course. I doubt this one will make the national society pages."

"Good," Grace said fervently.

"I hope Bryan will manage to enjoy himself. He won't know anyone, of course, and I'm not sure he's used to small-town society. We aren't exactly New

York City around here. Heck, we aren't even Little Rock.''

"Don't worry, Mom. Bryan has a good time wherever he goes. And he might have grown up rich, but he still grew up in Arkansas.''

"How is his arm? I've been so concerned about him.''

"He's healing just fine,'' Grace assured her, as she had the last two times she'd talked with her mother since Sunday.

"Did you see the new article in the state newspaper today? The interview with that woman whose children he saved? She thinks he's practically a saint. She went on and on about what a hero he was to risk his own life to save her babies. And she said he's called to check on them and he's sent gifts to the children. I'm sure the national media will jump on this story.''

"They already have. And they're probably embroidering it as we speak,'' Grace said wryly. "By the time the tabloids report it, Bryan will have saved a dozen kids and suffered grievous injuries, himself.''

"You're probably right,'' Evelyn agreed with a sigh.

"But Bryan really was a hero on Sunday,'' Grace added, for honesty's sake, and because she knew her mother would like hearing it. "I've never personally seen a braver act in my whole life.''

"Have the reporters been calling you to ask about what happened?''

"A few called. I've simply told them that I'm glad the children are okay, and that I'm also relieved Bryan wasn't seriously injured. Other than that, I have no comment—which frustrates them no end, of course.''

"I must say you're handling all this media attention better than I expected. I was afraid you might grow impatient with the silly speculation and lose that famous temper of yours."

"It's been a close call a few times," Grace admitted. "I just keep reminding myself that this is all for Chloe's sake."

"And you would do anything for your sister—just as she would for you." Evelyn obviously took great satisfaction from that observation about her children's loyalty to each other.

"I'd really better get back to work, Mom. Is there anything else you want to discuss before I go?"

"No. I just wanted to visit with you. I'll see you Friday."

"Yes. Friday."

"I love you, honey."

"Love you, too, Mom. Bye, now."

Grace hung up the phone, then hid her face in her hands. She had known from the beginning that this plan of Bryan's wasn't going to be easy. She just hadn't realized exactly how complicated it would be.

She hadn't understood how deeply involved she would become with her co-conspirator.

Chapter Ten

Grace was almost relieved when Bryan was summoned out of town for a business crisis late Wednesday afternoon. He called her at the shop to tell her he had to go, and to promise that he would be back in time for the party Friday evening.

"Are you sure you're up to making a trip like that?" Grace couldn't help asking.

His reply was tinged with exasperation. "Give me a break. A minor burn is hardly going to keep me bedridden. Despite your concerns—and Donovan's and Jason's—I'm perfectly capable of doing my job."

She knew that, of course. Even if he did tend to downplay his injuries, and to deny the discomfort he must still be feeling, there was no reason Bryan couldn't handle a routine business trip. And his being gone for a few days would give her a chance to get her feelings about him under control. She had trouble thinking clearly when he was too close.

"Take care of yourself," she said simply.

"You, too. And Grace…"

"Yes?"

"Promise me you won't try to ditch the security detail while I'm gone."

She groaned. "You're going to have me watched the whole time you're out of town?"

"Watched *over,*" he corrected her. "It will be public knowledge that I'll be in Seattle for the next couple of days. I'm not leaving you completely unprotected while I'm gone."

"I'll be perfectly safe. I've been watching out for myself for years."

"Yes, but that was before I came along to complicate your life," he reminded her. His cheerful tone didn't hide the fact that he had no intention of allowing her to change his mind.

"You got that right," she muttered.

"I'll miss you, Grace."

She frowned at the telephone, not sure if he was still teasing. He'd sounded serious that time. But he was a very talented actor, she reminded herself. "Well…um…have a good trip."

He sighed heavily, the humor back now. "I suppose it was too much to hope that you'd miss me, too. But that's okay. I'm not one to give up easily once I set my mind to something."

Now he was making her nervous. "Goodbye, Bryan."

"Bye, darling."

She hung up before he could add whatever blarney he came up with next. And, damn it, she *was* going to miss him.

"I hope Bryan gets here in time for the party." Evelyn Pennington looked out her living-room window for the seventh or eighth time in the past hour.

"He said he would do his best," Grace reminded her from a doily-decorated wing chair across the room. She glanced at her watch. "He still has nearly an hour to get here before we need to leave, and I gave him directions to the club if he misses us here."

"I'm sure he's trying his best." Patting her spray-stiffened silvery hair, Evelyn stepped away from the window. "Are you sure I can't get you anything, honey? Don't you want a soft drink before you change for the party?"

Grace shook her head. "There will be plenty to eat and drink once we get there."

A mixture of voices preceded three people into the room. Chloe, Donovan, and Hank Pennington had been out in the backyard to examine Hank's prized new bass boat, which Grace had already seen and dutifully admired.

"Bryan hasn't called?" Donovan asked Grace.

"No. I guess he's running a little late."

"I hope he hasn't been detained by a business problem," Chloe fretted.

The seemingly casual remark fell rather heavily into the room. Grace imagined the others were remembering the same thing she was. The last time Bryan had been detained on a business trip, he'd asked Donovan to give Chloe a lift to his vacation resort. Before Bryan had been able to join them there, Chloe and Donovan had been kidnapped.

Realizing what unpleasant memories she had unintentionally invoked, Chloe spoke again quickly. "I'd better go change for the party."

Grace stood. "Yeah, me, too."

Leaving Justin and Bob to close the shop, they had left early that afternoon, bringing their party clothes with them. Donovan's things had been stashed in Chloe's old room; Chloe and Grace would dress in Grace's former bedroom.

Grace and Chloe had both brought cool and cásual dresses for the party. It was nice to be able to dress comfortably for a change, Grace reflected as she buckled the strap of one low-heeled sandal. Her feet were particularly relieved.

"You're sure you're okay about tonight?" Chloe asked as she stood in front of the mirror, fastening her gold hoop earrings. "I know it will be awkward for you, having to pretend in front of everyone that you and Bryan are a couple."

"We've been participating in that pretense for several weeks now."

"Yes, but that was for strangers. This is different."

Since Grace had just been thinking very much along the same lines, she couldn't argue. "I'll get through it. We don't have to lie, really. Bryan and I have been dating—we don't have to explain why. We've never implied to anyone that we're engaged or even discussing a long-term relationship. All we have to do this evening is act like very good friends and answer any questions politely but vaguely."

"You and Bryan have become friends, haven't you? I've noticed that you seem to enjoy being together."

"Chloe..."

Her sister gave her an innocent look. "I'm not matchmaking. It was only an observation."

"Humph." Unconvinced, Grace stood and stepped to the mirror, and picked up the hairbrush that had been lying on the dressertop.

There was an eerie sense of déjà vu to getting dressed in her old bedroom with Chloe. Evelyn had changed the décor of the room during the past eleven years since Grace moved out, transforming it from a teenager's room to a guest room, but the furniture was the same. It didn't take much imagination for Grace to see the room as it once had been, decorated with beads and stuffed animals and posters of long-haired rock stars. Chloe's room had been "prissier"—lace and porcelain and Degas prints. The twins had always made an effort to express their individuality, and yet the bond between them had always been strong.

Things were changing, Grace mused wistfully. Not so long ago, she had been the most important person in her sister's life. She was fully aware that she had now taken second place. When Chloe and Donovan had children—and Chloe wanted them soon—Grace would slip even further down the priority scale. As it should be, of course. She and Chloe would always be close, but Chloe's first loyalty must be to her own family.

Evelyn's voice cut through Grace's temporary melancholy. "Grace, honey, there's a call for you. It's Bryan."

Chloe frowned. "I hope he isn't calling to say he can't make it. Donovan and I really want him to be with us this evening."

Grace didn't mention that she felt much the same way. As awkward as it would be for her to try to deceive her old friends and neighbors, she suspected that it would be even more problematic going to the party without Bryan. There would be questions about him to field, speculation about whether they'd broken up, concerned reminders about how quickly time passed for a single woman approaching her thirties. This was still an old-fashioned community in some ways. Women Grace's age were expected to be married—or at least putting a great deal of effort into attaining that goal.

She walked to the kitchen to take the call, since there was no extension in her old room. "Bryan?" she said while her mother hovered in the background, quietly unloading the dishwasher. "Is something wrong?"

"My plane was delayed a couple of hours in Dallas. I'm in Little Rock now, just leaving for Searcy. Do you want to wait for me there at your parents' house or should I join you at the party?"

Because she knew what her mother would want her to do, Grace answered, "You can join us there. Don't rush. There's no need to risk your life trying to get here too quickly."

"Okay. Sorry about the holdup."

"It isn't your fault. Are you having someone drive you?"

"I'm driving myself. My arm is much better, hardly even sore now. Jason picked me up at the airport and dropped me off at my place, so I've got the car."

Grace had convinced Donovan to return the Corvette to Bryan's house while Bryan was away, telling him—and herself—that there was no need for her to keep it any longer. "Be careful," she urged again.

"I will. See you soon, gorgeous."

For some stupid reason, she was blushing a little when she hung up the phone—and she was quite sure her sharp-eyed mother noticed. "Bryan's going to be a little late. He'll join us at the club."

"I'm glad he'll be able to come. How is his arm?"

"He said it's much better. It's probably still more sore than he'll admit, but he seems to be healing quickly."

"I'm glad to hear that." Evelyn studied Grace's black-and-white color-blocked sleeveless dress. "I like that outfit. Is it new?"

Grace lifted her arms and made an exaggerated runway model's turn. "Found it on a clearance rack."

"It's very flattering. I'm sure Bryan will like it."

Uh-oh. Not her mother, too. "Mom, don't forget Bryan and I are simply putting on an act to draw gossip away from Chloe and Donovan."

Grace knew now where Chloe had gotten that innocent-little-me expression she'd used earlier. Her hazel eyes wide, Evelyn said sweetly, "I know, honey. I was just making a comment about how pretty you look this evening."

"Right." Grace didn't believe her mother any more than she had her sister earlier. What was with her family today? Was the imaginary scent of orange blossoms clouding their thinking?

Surely they understood that she and Bryan were completely wrong for each other. Grace had no interest in sharing his social fishbowl, watching everything she said or did in case it appeared in a gossip column the next day. And Bryan was undoubtedly looking for someone more patient and biddable, more gracious and tactful than Grace. Someone like Chloe.

Hank marched into the kitchen, frowning at his watch. "Shouldn't we be going? We'll be late. Grace, where's your sister?"

Struck by nostalgia again—her compulsively punctual father had spent most of her life hurrying the family to one event or another—she smiled and said, "I bet she sneaked into Donovan's room."

Hank scowled. "Well, go tell them to hurry up. Folks are waiting for us."

She kissed his weathered cheek as she passed him. "Yes, Daddy."

There was already a good-sized crowd at the country club when they arrived, Grace following the others in her own car.

"See?" Hank muttered when they gathered outside the entrance door. "I told you we'd be late."

"We weren't expected to be the first ones here," Evelyn replied mildly. "Everyone will want to greet Chloe and Donovan when they enter."

Hank tugged at the tie his wife had made him wear. "Let's get this over with."

Donovan looked almost as enthusiastic as Hank at the prospect of the evening ahead. Grace sympathized with both men.

The ballroom had been decorated in white gauze and gold lamé. Gold and white balloons floated serenely above the floor. Creamy candles and magnolia blossoms filled nearly every available surface. Grace could see the hand of Cassie Barnum in the decorations. It had been Cassie who had decorated for every dance and homecoming party when they'd been in high school together. Since graduation, Cassie, now a florist and mother of three, had decorated numerous weddings, parties, pageants, proms and other local festivities.

Cassie rushed forward to greet them first. She had gained forty pounds or so since high school, but her smile was still bubbly and infectious. "Chloe!" she squealed, hugging her old classmate. "You look beautiful."

Chloe returned the warm squeeze, then motioned toward her fiancé. "Cassie Barnum, this is Donovan Chance."

Grace almost laughed at Donovan's expression when Cassie promptly threw her arms around him. She hoped Chloe had warned Donovan that their old friends tended to be a "huggy" bunch. He was going to be embraced by total strangers and welcomed like a long-lost son. For a reserved, undemonstrative man like Donovan, it was going to be a long evening.

While the rest of her family was surrounded by friends, Grace became the object of Cassie's attention. After the customary hug, Cassie asked, "Isn't Mr. Falcon going to be here this evening?"

"Bryan's been delayed. He'll be joining us shortly."

"Oh, good. I can't wait to meet him." Cassie leaned closer and lowered her voice to a conspiratorial whisper. "Is he really as handsome as he looks in photographs?"

"Better," Grace answered candidly, thinking of the impact of Bryan's beautiful blue eyes when seen up close and personal.

Cassie sighed. "Oh, my goodness. I just hope I don't embarrass myself by stammering when I meet him."

Grace's response was dry. "I'm sure he's used to it."

Within the next fifteen minutes, it seemed that everyone in the room had asked her where Bryan was. There was plenty of attention given to Chloe and Donovan, of course, but Bryan was considered the real celebrity. It wasn't every day that a man who had been discussed in *People, Forbes,* and *Newsweek* mingled among them. A man who had dated super-models, dined at the White House and hobnobbed with captains of industry. Not only that, he was a real-life hero who rescued small children in his free time.

Grace understood why her friends were so fasci-nated by Bryan. And why they were finding it so hard to imagine her dating such a man. She found that rather hard to believe, herself.

She stayed close to her parents as they worked the room, after discovering that people were less likely to get too personal about her relationship with Bryan when her mother and father were standing beside her. There were several comments about Chloe's new short hairstyle, and how much easier it was to tell the twins apart now.

"You girls still look just alike, though," her mother's old friend Elsie Carpenter remarked. "It's no wonder all those gossip columnists got the two of you mixed up."

It made it easier for Grace to keep playing the part of Bryan's "frequent companion" when she had such validation that the plan had been successful. Among their friends, at least, it seemed to be taken for granted that the media had been wrong, and that the couples had been paired off this way all along.

She was chatting with her old history teacher, Mrs.

Kinnelly, when a stir from the other side of the room caught her attention. Unless she was mistaken, her date had just arrived.

A moment later, she spotted him being escorted across the room by her mother. Evelyn clung to Bryan's right arm, looking so comfortable with him that one would have thought she'd known him forever rather than having met him only recently. "Look who finally made it," Evelyn sang out cheerily.

Her pulse racing through her veins, Grace cleared her throat in an attempt to make her voice sound normal when she greeted him. She could only assume that her sudden attack of nerves was due to the knowledge that everyone in the big room was watching them. It surely wasn't only excitement at seeing Bryan again—even if he did look spectacular in his pale-gray jacket, charcoal slacks and crisp white shirt. His bandages were hidden, and he looked completely healthy. His tie was a geometric print of grays and white, and had probably cost more than Grace's clearance-rack dress.

Cassie wasn't the only one who was in danger of stammering at the sight of him.

She was pleased that her voice came out steadily. "Hello, Bryan."

She should have been prepared for his next move—but she hadn't been. She was in his arms with his mouth on hers before she could brace herself for the impact.

The kiss didn't last long, but it still turned her knees to gelatin. She had to cling to his right arm for support when he finally drew back. She knew her cheeks were flaming. He'd kissed her right there in front of everyone—including her mother and her old history teacher!

She could tell from his wicked smile that he knew full well what he had done to her. "Hi, darling. Miss me?"

"Of course." She lifted her chin and gave him a look that ordered him to behave. "How was your trip?"

"Much too long." He turned his high-voltage smile on Mrs. Kinnelly, who was watching them avidly. "Hello. I'm Bryan Falcon."

Proving that even seventy-year-old women weren't immune to his charms, the retired teacher tittered a little as she replied, "I know who you are, of course. And I'm Helen Kinnelly."

"It's a pleasure to meet you, ma'am."

Mrs. Kinnelly smiled at Grace's mother. "Both of your daughters have found such polite young men, Evelyn. But I knew they would. You raised them well—even if Grace did raise a few eyebrows when she was a teenager."

His arm around Grace's shoulders, Bryan chuckled. "I've always admired women with spirit. I bet you raised a few eyebrows in your day, as well."

Mrs. Kinnelly blushed like one of the hundreds of schoolgirls she had taught during her career. "I got into my share of mischief."

Bryan winked at her and then turned to greet someone else who was trying to get his attention, leaving the older woman smiling and fanning her face with one hand.

"Can you believe this guy?" Grace asked her sister a short while later. "All he has to do is walk into a roomful of strangers and he suddenly has everyone eating out of his hands.''

Chloe looked across the room to the refreshments table where Bryan and Donovan had gone to fetch drinks. ''He really is amazing.''

Following her sister's gaze, Grace studied the two men. They made an impressive sight as they crossed the room, Bryan so sleek and polished, Donovan so solid and powerful. She doubted that many would have the courage to take them on.

There was no mistaking, in her opinion, who was the leader and who the second in command. Donovan seemed to walk a half-step behind Bryan, as if constantly guarding his back. Grace had never thought of herself as particularly drawn to powerful men—but she was definitely drawn to Bryan.

She wasn't the only one.

Cassie Barnum clutched her arm from behind. ''Oh. My. God,'' she murmured, staring at the men who had been delayed by conversation. ''You were right. The photos don't do him justice.''

Grace smiled. ''I know.''

''And he's obviously just crazy about you. You're so lucky.''

Grace's smile faded. Bryan was a very talented actor, she could have said—but, of course, she didn't. Bryan joined them before she had to come up with a reply. ''You aren't talking about me, are you, darling?''

Grace shrugged. ''Actually we were talking about balloons and other things that are filled with hot air. I think your name might have come up in the conversation.''

Cassie gasped, then giggled.

Knowing full well that he'd just been insulted, Bryan grinned and lifted his punch cup in an implied "touché." He turned then to Cassie, whom he'd met earlier. "Someone told me you're responsible for the lovely decorations this evening."

She beamed, then said modestly, "Of course it's nothing like you're used to seeing in New York and L.A."

Bryan assured her that he much preferred simplicity to ostentatiousness. Grace simply stood back and watched in resignation as he made another fan for life.

The more Bryan impressed Grace's friends, the more they seemed to become convinced that she should make sure she didn't let him get away. Donovan was unanimously approved as a mate for Chloe; and everyone seemed to agree that Bryan suited Grace.

She lost count of the number of times she was asked if Bryan had proposed to her yet. She found it especially ironic that many seemed convinced they were waiting to announce their engagement because they didn't want to draw attention away from Chloe and Donovan. She wondered what those same people would have said if she informed them that she and Bryan were together specifically to draw attention away from the other couple.

The trapped feeling was growing in her again— trapped in a lie, and in a future that seemed to hold little excitement. It became more of an effort to keep socializing, to keep smiling and chatting and blithely deflecting personal questions.

She thought she was doing a pretty good job of hiding her real emotions. Though she didn't try to convince herself she was as good at that sort of thing as Bryan, everyone appeared convinced that she was having a lovely time at the party. Even her family seemed unconcerned. She should have known it wouldn't be so easy to deceive a master deceiver.

"Need to get out of here for a while?" Bryan asked in her ear.

She turned her head to find him standing very close to her, his expression entirely too knowing. "I don't think we can leave yet," she whispered. "There are going to be some speeches made for Chloe and Donovan later and it will be rude if we leave before hearing them."

"We could step outside for a few minutes. You can show me the gardens—maybe even scream a little, if you need to."

She laughed at the thought of the attention a loud, unexpected scream would attract. "That would liven things up."

"At least your smile is real now," he observed, eyeing her in satisfaction. "Come show me the gardens."

The temptation to get out of this room, if only for a few minutes, was simply too great. She turned to her mother. "Bryan and I are going to step outside for some fresh air. We won't be long, but send someone for us if the speeches start before we get back, okay?"

Evelyn smiled. "I wondered how long it would be before you would have to escape."

So apparently she hadn't fooled her mother very well, either. Was she really fooling *anybody?*

Grace was aware of the eyes that followed their path toward the exit doors. Everyone probably thought she and Bryan wanted to be alone because he had been out of town for a couple of days. They would be surreptitiously checking out her hair and makeup when she returned, imagining invisible handprints all over her body.

She didn't care what they thought. She had to get out. She was suddenly having trouble breathing in here.

They passed a crowd of older men swapping fishing lies in the lobby—Grace spotted her father among them—and then walked through the outside doors into the warm August evening. A group of smokers clustered under the awning just outside the door. Grace held her breath as she walked quickly through the cloud of smoke, merely nodding in response to their greetings.

Softly lit paths crisscrossed the gardens behind the club building. Planted with ornamental trees, rosebushes and a variety of other blooming plants, the gardens lay between the club and the golf course. Moonlight washed the landscape in a soft glow, glittering off the small lake in the center of the golf course. The scent of roses surrounded them, pleasantly replacing the smell of cigarette smoke.

A night for romance, Grace mused. And the perfect companion to share it with, she added with a sideways glance at Bryan.

Be very careful, Grace.

Bryan led her to a small bench set in a shadowy grotto formed by two spreading, lacy-leafed Japanese maples. The bench was just large enough to hold them both; he sat on her left so that his good arm was next to her. "This is nice, isn't it?"

She nodded. "I needed to get away from the crowd for a few minutes."

"I could tell."

She wrinkled her nose. "Was I that obvious about it?"

"Not to everyone else, perhaps. But I must admit I was watching you rather closely."

Because that comment made her self-conscious, she looked away from him. "I'm glad you were able to make it tonight. Chloe would have been disappointed if you couldn't come."

He ran his fingertips lightly down her bare arm. "Is Chloe the only one who would have been disappointed?"

Grace cleared her throat. "I'm sure Donovan is glad you're here, so he isn't the only one having to deal with so many strangers."

A faintly reproving note entered his voice. "You mean you wouldn't have missed me at all?"

"I'm glad you're here," she admitted. Then, when his hand closed over hers, she backtracked quickly. "It's nice to have an excuse to escape the crowd."

"I'll take that as a compliment—whether it was intended as one or not."

His fingers were intertwined with hers now, their hands resting on his knee. Holding her hand in a moonlit rose garden. Creating a memory of a perfect romantic moment. She might never forgive him for this.

Chapter Eleven

Grace slanted a look up at Bryan, only to find him studying her face. His face was shadowed by the moon behind him, but she could see his eyes, steady and clear. "You really are lovely," he murmured.

"I look just like Chloe," she answered gruffly.

"You do, of course. And yet there's still a difference. Even when you wore your hair the same way, I could always tell you apart."

She couldn't really doubt him. It had always surprised her that he could tell them apart so easily, from the first time he'd met them. More than once he had breezed into the shop, taken one glance at her before she'd had a chance to say a word, and said, "Hello, Grace."

There were people who had known them for years who still couldn't identify them with just a glance.

She clearly remembered those first few times when

he'd strolled into the shop, his thick black hair wind-blown, his bright blue eyes gleaming, his cheeks a bit reddened because it had been winter when he'd first started coming around. Every time she had seen him, her heart had shown an infuriating tendency to flip over in her chest. Because she had known each time that he was there to see Chloe, she had greeted him with frowns and growls.

She'd told herself she didn't trust this slick-talking, sweet-smiling playboy millionaire as far as she could throw him. She didn't like him hanging around her sister, and she nearly went ballistic when Chloe confided in her that Bryan had been talking of marriage only weeks after he and Chloe first met. Apparently he had developed a prosaic list of qualifications for a bride, and Chloe met nearly every one.

Chloe had briefly considered taking Bryan up on that offer. She'd told Grace that she would be foolish not to at least consider it. She wanted marriage and children, and she had found a nice, successful, financially secure man who wanted the same things. Chloe hadn't fallen in love with Bryan—nor, she'd added, did he ever claim to be in love with her—but they had become very good friends.

Grace hadn't bothered to closely examine her own passionate opposition to Bryan's calculated courtship of her sister. She had simply insisted that it was wrong, that Chloe deserved better than to be married because she fit some esoterically compiled profile. She'd pointed out Bryan's widely recorded history of short-lived relationships, and had asked Chloe what made her think he would stay with her any longer than he had the others. She'd been convinced that Chloe would end up disappointed, disillusioned, and very publicly humiliated when he lost interest in her and moved on to someone else—another supermodel, perhaps.

She had been prickly and surly and outright rude to Bryan when he'd dated her sister. He had been unfailingly patient and courteous to her in return. Which, of course, had only made her more disagreeable.

And now he had turned his attentions to her. She looked down at their clasped hands and frowned. This just wasn't right.

She made an effort to pull her hand away from his. "We should be getting back inside."

He didn't immediately release her. "What's your hurry? We've only been out here a few minutes."

"Yes, well, I don't want to be gone too long. People might notice."

"They'll probably assume we're out here enjoying a few kisses in the moonlight. Which is pretty much what we want them to think, isn't it?"

She cleared her throat and tugged at her hand again. "Donovan would probably appreciate it if you'd go back inside and talk to him. I can tell he's getting a little stressed out by being examined and interrogated by so many people."

"Donovan's a big boy. He can take care of himself." Bryan lifted her hand to his lips and brushed a kiss against her knuckles. "Don't you like being out here with me, Grace?"

The caress made her shiver. And because that made her mad, she snatched her hand away. "I don't want you to do that anymore."

"What? Kiss your hand?"

"No. I mean, yes. That, too. *Any* kisses. It has to stop."

"Is that right?"

She sprang to her feet. "Do not be all calm and soothing and polite to me. It drives me crazy when you do that."

He laid his right arm along the back of the bench and gazed up at her. "I'm sorry. Would you like me to be agitated and impolite?"

"And don't patronize me. I really hate it when you do that."

He rose and took a step closer to her. Standing with the moon behind him, he looked tall and dark and a little intimidating. She almost moved back a step, but wouldn't give up that much pride. "What's going on, Grace?"

"Nothing. I just think this is all getting out of hand. Reality is getting mixed up with fantasy, and I don't like it. And this is entirely the wrong time and place to discuss it, anyway, because anyone could come out here and overhear us and then all our efforts would have been wasted."

"You're right," he agreed. She couldn't see his face, but his tone was somber. "This isn't the time or place. But we do need to talk. Soon."

Definitely something she wanted to avoid. "There's really nothing to say. We both know our parts. We both know what's going to happen after the wedding. Why complicate things?"

He reached up to touch his fingertips to her flushed cheek. "It's already gotten complicated."

"Then we have to...what now?"

He had dropped his hands on her shoulders and was pulling her closer. "Someone's coming," he murmured. ''Don't want to be caught squabbling, do we?''

"I really don't—"

She stopped in resignation when he kissed her. No one could accuse Bryan of not fully playing his role. In fact, he kissed her with much more enthusiasm than was necessary to fool an incidental bystander. His mouth moved firmly on hers, warm and insistent, giving her little chance to resist. Or even to respond.

There was a new element to this kiss, she noted even as her mind began to cloud with that now-familiar haze. Not quite anger—but a new assertiveness that was very likely a response to her efforts to take control of their temporary relationship.

As she had feared, Bryan wasn't going to be co-operative. She shouldn't have been surprised, she supposed. He'd been a challenge to her since she'd first met him.

He lifted his head, took a quick breath, then kissed her again before she could step away. She couldn't help responding this time, if only a little. Only for the sake of whoever was watching, she assured herself as her eyelids drifted downward. She would not be the one to ruin everything they had accomplished during the past weeks.

The undercurrents of irritation were gone now. Bryan's lips moved more gently on hers, more persuasively. Clinging to the lapels of his jacket, she tilted her head a bit more to one side, changing the angle of the embrace. Much better, she decided.

She didn't know quite how much time passed before Bryan finally drew back. She was chagrined to realize that he was the one who ended the kiss, without any urging from her. She blinked a couple of times—had the moon suddenly gotten brighter?—then looked around. "I don't see anyone else here."

"My mistake," he murmured and disentangled her hands from his jacket so he could step back.

She scowled at him, wondering if he'd ever really heard anything. Or had he been trying to prove his point that they had already crossed the line between playacting and actuality? "Damn it, Bryan—"

He glanced at the luminous dial of his watch. "We'd better go back inside for the speeches. We'll finish our talk later."

As far as Grace was concerned, their talk was over. She hoped he'd gotten her message—but she had a feeling it had fallen on deliberately deaf ears.

It wasn't possible for Grace to avoid Bryan for the remainder of the party, of course—not without arousing curiosity in the other guests. She stayed close to his side, smiled at him and chatted with him, doing her best to look like one half of a very happy couple.

Chloe and Donovan were called to the front of the room, where Chloe looked radiant and Donovan uncomfortable as one old friend after another stood to wish the couple well in their marriage. A local videographer taped the entire proceedings as a gift for the couple. Grace held on to her bright smile even when several broad hints about the joys of wedlock were aimed directly at her and Bryan. She really should be nominated for some sort of acting award this evening.

Whenever the strain became too great, she had only to look at Chloe to remind herself why she was doing this. Chloe looked so happy. Even Donovan, beneath his embarrassment, seemed to almost radiate contentment. He didn't exactly wear his heart on his sleeve, but every time he looked at Chloe, it was obvious to anyone with only a modicum of perception that he was deeply in love with her. He wasn't acting—Grace had no doubt that Donovan's feelings for her sister were real and lasting.

She was delighted for her twin. She really was. She believed that fate had brought Chloe and Donovan together, and she hoped they would share a long, happy life. She said something along those lines when she was pressed into giving her own brief speech for the couple.

Bryan's words were saved for last. He took the microphone with the ease of someone who was quite comfortable speaking in front of crowds.

"My parents had only one child," he said, smiling at Donovan, "but fate brought me a brother several years ago. Now my honorary brother is getting married, giving me an honorary sister. I look forward to spoiling several honorary nieces and nephews. There's an old Irish blessing that seems particularly suitable this evening. Chloe and Donovan, 'May God go with you and bless you. May you see your children's children. May you be poor in misfortune and rich in blessings. And may you know nothing but happiness from this day forward.'"

She should definitely receive some sort of award, Grace mused again, her smile stretched across her face as she applauded along with everyone else. If there was a tear in her eye, she knew it would be attributed to sentimental joy for her sister. Which, of course, was the only reason she felt the urge to cry, she assured herself.

What else could it be?

* * *

Because Grace had brought her own car, she had the drive home to herself. Bryan insisted on following her since it was rather late when the party ended. She was aware of his headlights in the rearview mirror all the way, but at least she didn't have to try to make conversation with him during the ride. She tuned the radio to a classic rock station, turned the volume up, and let the beat of the bass drown out her thoughts.

Bryan parked beside her in the garage. She was already out of her car before he could turn off his engine. "There's no need to come up," she told him as he opened his car door. "It's late, and I'm sure you're tired after your trip."

"I thought we were going to talk."

Clutching her things to her chest, she took a step backward. "Maybe you aren't tired, but I am. I've been running all day and I have to work tomorrow."

He must have seen the desperation in her face—or heard it, perhaps, in her voice. He didn't press her this time, merely saying, "All right. Get some rest. We'll talk later."

"Right. Later."

Much later, she told herself as she turned and hurried toward the elevator. Much, *much* later.

If she was lucky, that was one potentially awkward talk that she would be able to avoid for a long time.

Grace disappeared again Saturday night.

While it didn't particularly surprise him this time, Bryan was still furious that she would take such a risk again after implying that she wouldn't. He wasn't as worried this time that someone had grabbed her on the way home from work; he had no doubt that she had deliberately taken off again. Maybe just to prove to him that she could.

He never should have eased back on security, but he'd thought he'd made his point to her about being extremely careful during the next few weeks. He hadn't expected her to ignore his warnings.

Aside from his very real concern for her safety, what was really eating at him was the question of who she was with. Picturing her with another man made a wave of fury crash through him, clenching his fists and tensing his muscles.

They were going to have to talk soon. *Very* soon. He needed to make it clear that as far as he was concerned, the playacting was over. He meant everything he said to her now—whether she chose to listen or not. He needed to make sure she understood that. And he needed very badly to find out if he was only imagining that she was having as much trouble separating fantasy from reality as he was. Hadn't she said those very words in the garden outside the country club last night?

Was she really so opposed to the possibility that something could be developing between them? Was her disappearing act this evening a panicky reaction to the tension that had been building every time they were together?

He considered breaking into her apartment again, being there to confront her at whatever hour she came dragging in. He would demand to know where she had been, and refuse to leave until he had a satisfactory answer. She would be furious, of course. There would be a heated shouting match, which would allow him, at least, to vent some steam.

But he was getting to know Grace very well. She

was looking for excuses to push him away, and he didn't want to give her any more at the moment. He was going to find out what was going on with her, but he wouldn't accomplish anything by fighting her. Not just yet, anyway.

Instructing his security detail to let him know when Grace was safely home, he prepared to spend the hours until he received that call pacing the carpets of his house.

He'd always considered himself a man of great patience—but Grace could try the patience of a saint. And he was definitely no saint. If he ever got his hands on her again, he would prove it.

Grace was expecting Bryan's call Sunday. She had half expected to find him waiting in her apartment when she'd gotten home at just after 1:00 a.m.

Since she didn't believe for a minute that she had managed to slip away without him being notified, she was fully prepared for another lecture from him. She even rather looked forward to it. She'd been practicing her own responses all day. Such as how he had no right to ask her where she went or what she did. How hard she had been working to make his crazy plan work out, and how she deserved an occasional break from the pressure of that charade.

She almost hoped he *would* start something. It was easier to fight with Bryan than to hold hands in the moonlight with him. She was more comfortable yelling at him; she knew what to do, what to say, and how to bring it to an end. She could slam down the phone or turn and storm away—actions she did well from experience.

She didn't hear from him until late Sunday. She

thought maybe he had called while she was at church, but there were no messages on her answering machine when she returned home after lunching with a few friends from her Sunday School class. Feeling as if she were waiting for a shoe to drop, she spent the next couple of hours doing laundry, cleaning her apartment, replacing a missing button on one of her favorite blouses. Just typical weekend chores—and yet she kept listening for the phone to ring or someone to knock on her door.

For some reason, the longer Bryan waited to contact her, the more annoyed she became. She *knew* he was aware that she'd been out last night. She knew he was going to chew her out about it. Why didn't he just go ahead and do it?

By the time the phone finally rang early that evening, her nerves were a bit frayed—as he probably knew they would be, the rat. She answered the phone with a clipped, "Hello."

There was a momentary hesitation, and then Bryan asked pleasantly, "Is this a bad time?"

"Not really," she said, setting aside the book she had just opened. Might as well get this over with.

"How has your weekend been?" he asked, the question sounding casual.

She shifted in her chair. "Fine, thank you. And yours?"

"Nothing special. I've been catching up on some work."

"Same here." Okay, could this conversation *get* more stilted and banal?

"Did you have a nice lunch with your church friends today? I understand you tried out the new Tex-Mex place. I've heard it's good."

"Yes, it's—wait a minute." Annoyed with herself for being so slow on the uptake, she pounded her fist on her knee. "Darn it, Bryan, you're having me followed again."

"Only since one o'clock this morning. I'm glad he was inconspicuous about it. I've given instructions for the security people to stay close, but to keep out of your way."

"And just how often am I being followed?"

"As of one o'clock this morning, they're operating on three eight-hour shifts."

"I'm being watched twenty-four hours a day?"

"Discreetly. You'll hardly notice."

Her hand gripped the receiver so tightly that the muscles in her arm quivered. "You have no right to do this."

His answer surprised her. "You're probably right. I suppose I am crossing the line by assigning bodyguards to you against your will."

"Then why—?"

"Because Wallace Childers has disappeared again," he cut in bluntly. "We don't know where he is or what he's up to, and I won't be comfortable about your safety until we know whether he's in this country."

"When did this happen?" she asked, just a bit skeptically.

"We had a report on him last Thursday. It was believed he was still in Mexico. The authorities there were closing in on him, but then he simply disappeared. The guy is slime, Grace, and he hates me. You know that. If he thought he could hurt me by hurting you, he would do so."

As angry as she was about his methods, it was hard

to yell at him for trying to protect her. Even if she did think he was overreacting. Even if she did believe he was being arrogant and high-handed in making decisions on her behalf without consulting her. Even if she did have a secret suspicion that he was more annoyed about her taking off without his permission than he was worried about Wallace Childers.

While she appreciated the concern he expressed for her, she would not apologize for clinging to the last remnants of her privacy. This collaboration would end in a few very weeks, and she would then have to go on as a single businesswoman facing her thirtieth birthday and trying to decide what to do with the rest of her life.

"I'll be careful," she told him. "Even though I sincerely doubt that Childers is going to show up here, I'll use common sense."

"The bodyguards will leave you alone," he promised. "They won't interfere with any of your plans. But I'm going to have to insist that they watch over you for the next few weeks. Think of it as another measure to make sure nothing interferes with the wedding."

Low blow. She sighed, knowing that further argument would serve no purpose. She had known when she'd impulsively slipped off again last night that there would be repercussions. Bryan had been adamant from the beginning about the need for security as long as they were pretending to be lovers. And since Chloe *had* been kidnapped just for being associated with him, Grace couldn't even accuse him of having no justification for his paranoia.

"I'll be glad when this wedding is over so we can bring an end to all this," she grumbled.

After a rather lengthy pause, he replied, "I'm sorry this has been so difficult for you."

His tone was a bit stiff—as if, perhaps, she had hurt his feelings. And now she felt guilty on top of everything else. She hadn't even realized she *could* hurt his feelings with a careless remark. "What I meant was…"

"Never mind. Now that we've gotten the security issue out of the way—once again—there's something else I need to discuss with you. It's a favor, actually, so feel free to decline."

"What sort of favor?" she asked warily.

"It concerns my parents. There was an article in a national business journal last Friday comparing my business style to my father's. The writer implied that my parents and I have been estranged since I went into business for myself. There was even a throwaway comment that my parents are elitists who don't approve of my current relationship with a mere shopkeeper."

"That would be me, I presume?"

"I'm afraid so. Anyway, as you know, I was quite busy Friday finishing up my business in Seattle and getting back to the party in Searcy, and I never had a chance to see the article. Apparently my father just got around to reading it this morning. He was outraged by the assertion that he resents me because I'm a better businessman than he is. He phoned my mother, who took great offense at being labeled a snob. Even though she is, and she's well aware of it."

Shaking her head at his matter-of-fact description of his parents, she asked, "So what's the favor you want to ask me?"

"My parents want us to have dinner with them tomorrow evening. I'm quite sure they'll make arrangements for a society reporter to just happen to wander by with a camera during the meal, at which time my father will make a grand gesture like toasting our happiness with my mother smiling mistily at us from his side. It will be an excruciatingly uncomfortable meal, but it won't last more than a couple of hours at most. Will you go?"

"You *want* to go?" Grace asked in disbelief.

"I would rather have a root canal. Without anesthesia."

Now she was really confused. "So why are you asking me?"

"Because they're the only parents I have," he answered simply. "The article embarrassed them, and they've asked me to help them counteract it. They rarely ask me for anything, so I don't mind doing them a favor every once in a while."

How could she turn him down after that, even if she was still annoyed with him? Although she'd almost rather have oral surgery herself, than to participate in a just-for-show dinner with Bryan's difficult parents, she supposed she could suffer through it as a favor to him. He had gone to so much effort to make it to the party for Chloe and Donovan Friday evening, and he'd been nothing but polite and gracious to her parents and their friends.

This guy was something else, she thought with a shake of her head. During the course of this one phone call, she'd gone from being furious at him for his arrogance to admiring him for his thoughtfulness.

"All right. What time are you picking me up?"

"You'll do it?" He sounded surprised.

Had he really doubted that she would? "Yes, I'll go."

"Thanks, Grace. That's very nice of you."

Even though he couldn't see her, she shrugged. "I just get tired of the gossip—even in business magazines, which should be above that sort of thing. Your relationship with your parents is nobody's business but yours."

"I agree."

She didn't add that she found his filial sense of obligation rather touching, especially considering the pain his self-absorbed parents must have caused him in the past. Not for the first time, she was grateful for the family she had. Her sister, of course, and their parents who might not have been wealthy or socially prominent, but had always provided them with whatever they needed in addition to unconditional love and support.

So she would have dinner with Bryan and his parents. After that would come the wedding, and then a few more very public dates. They would keep the act going for a few weeks after the wedding, and then they would bring it to an amicable end, answering media questions with vague smiles and polite "no comments."

And then it would be over. As it had to be, she assured herself. No regrets.

Yeah, right, Grace.

Chapter Twelve

"It wasn't quite as bad as a root canal, I suppose," Bryan murmured as he drove Grace home from the exclusive downtown restaurant where they had spent the past two very long hours.

Grace ran her tongue experimentally over her teeth. She had never had a root canal, but she wasn't sure it could be much worse than dinner with Bryan's parents. Her cheeks still ached from the fake smile she'd worn all during the meal. It hadn't been easy—especially when his father continuously spoke to her as if she had the IQ of an average five-year-old and his mother asked a string of utterly inane questions about the shop.

Normally she would have let anyone else know exactly what she thought of their patronizing behavior. But these were Bryan's parents. She had restrained herself for his sake—and because she had solemnly promised Chloe that she would behave.

It had been a struggle, but she'd managed. She was rather proud of herself, actually. And thoroughly relieved that she would never have to go through that again.

"You really were great this evening," Bryan commented, proving that he'd been thinking along the same lines. "I know it wasn't easy for you."

"It wasn't too bad."

He laughed and reached over to give her a companionable pat on the knee, through the thin fabric of her summery, light-colored slacks. "You're a liar. But I still appreciate what you did tonight."

"I just hope we accomplished something. Except for the photographer who stopped by our table to snap a photo of your father toasting us—you predicted that to the last detail, by the way—no one seemed to pay much attention to us."

"Don't you believe it. Nearly everyone there saw us and recognized us. The ones who didn't were informed of our identify by the serving staff and other diners."

"And you think they'll talk about seeing us all together?"

"Oh, yeah. They'll suspect the dinner was specifically arranged for tonight because of that journal article, but it was obvious that we were all being pleasant and cordial. We might not have looked like a Norman Rockwell family, but we obviously aren't estranged, either."

His hand was still on her knee. Grace picked it up and set it firmly on the steering wheel. "Are you ever going to tell your parents why you and I have been seen together so often during the past few weeks? That we aren't really a couple?''

Still grinning at the byplay with his hand, he shrugged. ''Probably not. They aren't really that interested in my social life. Who I see, or why. Unless, of course, there's a chance that I could introduce Mother to someone from Hollywood. You know how she feels about anyone who's ever been on a movie screen.''

''Yes, she makes that clear enough.'' It hadn't escaped Grace that his parents hadn't even asked how his injuries were healing. She hoped they had asked during telephone calls, at least, or had expressed some concern for their son's well-being. After a moment, she asked a question that had been bothering her all evening. ''How did you end up so different from your parents?''

He shrugged again. ''I didn't spend a whole lot of time with them. I was raised by a series of nannies and housekeepers. Spent some time with my paternal grandmother until she died when I was eleven. Mostly I just raised myself.''

She would *not* feel sorry for him, she told herself. It would be a tremendous waste of time to feel sorry for Bryan Falcon. Instead she said merely, ''You spoiled yourself rotten.''

He laughed. ''You aren't the first to say that.''

He pulled into the parking space next to her car and killed the engine. ''Are you going to ask me up for coffee, or are you going to bolt again?''

She gave it only a moment's thought. ''I'm going to bolt,'' she said, unbuckling her seat belt and reaching for the door handle.

He caught her arm, holding her in her seat. ''What

are you so afraid of, Grace? What do you think will happen if I come up?"

"We'll fight," she said promptly. "You'll start lecturing me again about how reckless and irresponsible I am when it comes to the security measures you want me to take, and that will make me mad and we'll start yelling at each other."

"What if I promise not to fight with you? We've already settled the issue of security as far as I'm concerned."

"Right. You have someone following me twenty-four hours a day whether I like it or not, and I'm supposed to accept that without complaint."

"Exactly. So there's nothing to fight about, right?"

"If you say so," she muttered.

"Which brings us to what you're *really* afraid of—that we won't fight."

She scowled at his hand on her arm. "Wanna bet?"

Ignoring her, he continued, "You're afraid we'll be alone up there together—not fighting—and things will start getting intense again."

"That's not—"

He reached out with his free hand to slide his fingers beneath her chin and turn her face toward him. "We'd start kissing again—and you'd enjoy it. Again. And that scares you all the way down to your toes."

"You obviously had too much wine with dinner," she said, trying to sound haughty instead of panicky. "It's gone straight to your head."

"I had half a glass because my father ordered a wine he knows I don't like. You know I'm right, Grace."

"About the wine? How could I know—?"

''About the kisses,'' he interrupted with strained patience. ''That's what really scares you, isn't it?''

''I'm not afraid of you, Bryan.''

His face was very close to hers now. ''Then maybe you're afraid of your own feelings.''

''That's ridicu—''

The man had an exasperating habit of kissing her right in the middle of her sentences. She had swallowed so many words lately, she'd probably gained an extra pound or two. He made her so darned crazy that she wrapped her arms around his neck and almost angrily kissed him back.

Twisting in his seat, he enveloped her in an embrace that nearly squeezed all the air from her lungs. His mouth was hard and demanding on hers. There was nothing tentative about this kiss, no holding back on either side.

Bryan had always been very careful to control his hands when he kissed her before; this time he let them roam. And, oh, was he good with them!

Her loose summer top proved no hindrance to his explorations. For the first time, she felt the heat of his palms on the bare skin of her sides and her back. And when his hands slipped between them and moved upward, her breasts ached to feel his touch there, as well.

She had fantasized about having him touch her more often than she cared to admit, dreamed of making love with him more times than she could remember. And he was absolutely right—it scared her senseless.

Because she had also fantasized about touching him, and because this seemed like the perfect opportunity to do so, she unlocked her arms from around his neck and slid them down his chest. Her fingers flexed against him, testing the solid feel of him, and she marveled again that he was more firmly muscled than his slender build would indicate at first glance.

Her imagination was definitely in high gear now, as she imagined how he would feel beneath his finely tailored clothes.

She shuddered when his hands finally closed over her breasts, his thumbs moving lazily, yet skillfully, over the thin fabric of her bra. A sound escaped her, muffled by his mouth against hers.

Excitement and a growing need for oxygen were making her dizzy. She clutched at his forearms, and she couldn't have said whether her intent was to pull his hands away or to hold them more tightly against her.

This time it was Bryan who made a choked sound. She knew immediately that it was not a murmur of pleasure. Realizing that she was tightly gripping his left forearm—she could feel the bandages beneath his jacket sleeve—she gasped, tore her mouth from beneath his, and immediately dropped her hands. "I hurt your arm. I'm so sorry—"

Shaking his head, he steadied her when she would have jerked away from him. "It's okay," he said. "You just happened to brush against the only small part of my arm that's still a little raw. It was an accident, and no damage was done. I hardly even feel it now."

She felt terrible that she had gotten so carried away with her own sensations that she'd forgotten about his injuries. "Are you sure you're all right? Maybe you should—"

''Grace,'' he cut in firmly, ''I'm fine. Really. It was just a twinge.''

Hastily rearranging her clothes, she wondered how on earth everything had gotten so out of hand. Hadn't they been arguing? Hadn't she been intent on getting out of this car and safely locked inside her apartment to avoid any more kisses or serious conversation? Hadn't she told herself before she'd left for this dinner tonight that if Bryan did try to kiss her again, she would let him know firmly and finally that she wasn't interested?

So much for even trying to pretend that she was completely unaffected by his kisses.

Bryan shifted back into his own seat, carefully lifting himself away from the gearshift that must have been digging into him during their embrace. ''I think I'm getting too old for make-out sessions in a sports car,'' he murmured. ''Maybe I should buy a mini-van.''

Her hands were shaking when she lifted them to her tumbled hair. ''Don't bother on my behalf. This is not going to happen again.''

''You're probably right. From now on, we'd better keep our kisses behind closed doors. We never know when a tabloid photographer might pop up.''

She groaned at the thought of seeing a front-page tabloid snapshot of herself and Bryan groping each other in his car. And then, after processing everything he had said, she shook her head. ''That's not what I meant. From now on, unless it's necessary for the sake of our public act, there will be no more kisses. Period.''

''And why is that?'' he asked genially.

''Because there's no purpose in it. No future to it.

You and I will be going our separate ways in a few weeks, and I'm not interested in a temporary dalliance during that time.''

''And if I were to reply that I'm not interested in a temporary dalliance, either?''

Was he implying that he was thinking long-term? That he wasn't planning to disappear from her life when the wedding was behind them and the need for deception was no longer an issue?

If so, he needed to be set straight about that, too. ''Then I would say, good. I'm glad you aren't going to be giving me any problems.''

He studied her in a way that made her wonder if he could see the nerves shimmering just beneath the surface of her deliberately stern expression. ''I'm not sure you understood what I meant.''

''Maybe *you're* the one who isn't understanding,'' she countered.

''And maybe we should wait and have this discussion another time. After the wedding, perhaps, when some of the pressure is off.''

The only thing she intended to say to him after the wedding was, ''So long, Bryan. It's been interesting.''

Keeping that thought to herself, she reached for her door handle. ''I'll see you Friday night at the rehearsal. I'll be pretty busy until then.''

''I understand. You need some time to think about what's happening between us.''

''*Nothing is*—'' She stopped and drew a deep breath, aware that nothing would be accomplished by an argument now. Not while her emotions—and presumably his—were still running so high. ''Good night, Bryan.''

''Good night, Grace.'' He didn't offer to walk her

up, most likely because he knew she would refuse. She grimly suspected that he would know when she arrived safely at her door. He probably had someone posted in her hallway to report to him.

She climbed out of the car and started to close the door behind her. With a sigh, she paused and looked back inside. "Are you okay to drive? Your arm, I mean."

His smile made her sorry she'd given in to the impulse to ask. Obviously he'd misinterpreted her very natural concern. "I'll be fine, darling. But thank you for asking."

She stepped away from the car and shut the door firmly. She didn't slam it—no matter how irritated she was with Bryan, she couldn't bring herself to mistreat that beautiful vehicle—but she made her frustration clear. And then she turned on one heel and marched toward the elevator, her chin high, her shoulders squared.

"Do a guy a favor and look where it gets me," she muttered beneath her breath, stabbing at the call button with her forefinger. "I sat through that gosh-awful boring meal with his parents, I smiled for that stupid photographer so they could pretend to be a happy family and what do I get for my kindness and generosity? A headache, that's what!"

Massaging her temples, she stepped into the elevator and leaned against the back wall. It wasn't only her head that ached, she thought with a scowl, rubbing at another ache in the center of her chest. And that was one pain she was afraid would only get worse during the next few days.

Donovan was unbelievably calm on his wedding day. Bryan watched his friend in amazement, wondering why he wasn't sweating or stammering or something.

Bryan knew his old buddy didn't like dressing up or being the focus of attention. And yet here he was, dressed in a tux and preparing to step out in front of a church full of people—and he didn't even look nervous.

He actually looked happier than Bryan had ever seen him.

"You're sure you want to go through with this, Donovan?" Jason Colby asked as he adjusted the sleeves of his own tuxedo jacket. "I can smuggle you out of here before anybody catches on."

Donovan chuckled. "Thanks, but I haven't changed my mind. I'm staying."

Jason heaved a heavy sigh and looked at Bryan. "She's brainwashed him, boss. Got him thinking he *wants* to give up his freedom."

"I'm thinking Donovan's not giving up anything. But he's gaining a hell of a lot."

Jason groaned. "Damn. You've been brainwashed, too. Next thing I know, you'll be buckling a ball and chain around your own ankle."

Smiling a little in response to his security chief's broad Texas drawl, Bryan thought of how closely he had come to standing in Donovan's shoes. Twice he had proposed marriage, and twice his plans had fallen through. Now he couldn't imagine himself waiting at the end of an aisle for either of the women he had considered marrying before, not even as fond as he was of Chloe.

He supposed he should consider himself lucky to have avoided making such a monumental mistake.

The minister entered the room, tapping his watch. "It's time to line up, gentlemen. We'll walk into the sanctuary together as soon as the organist gives us the signal."

Bryan was amused that Donovan stepped forward so quickly. "I'm ready," he said.

The minister smiled. "I see that you are."

Bryan and Jason fell into step behind their friend. A short time later, they stood together in front of the church. Groom, best man, and groomsman, standing straight and stiff in their tuxedoes as they waited for the ceremony to begin.

Bryan didn't know many of the guests, only a few business associates of his and Donovan's. Chloe's family and friends and members of her church made up the rest of the cozy assemblage. Her mother was already sniffling into a lace-edged handkerchief. She happened to catch his eyes; he winked at her, eliciting a watery smile.

The little flower girl, the five-year-old daughter of one of Chloe's cousins, came down the aisle dropping rose petals from a beribboned basket. Her angelic face was creased in an adorable frown of concentration. There was no ring bearer; the rings were stashed securely in Bryan's pocket. At least, he hoped they were…

A quick, discreet exploration reassured him that the rings were exactly where they were supposed to be. He gave a small sigh of relief and turned his attention back to the wedding procession.

Another cousin of Chloe's, Angie Parrish, served as bridesmaid, her curly red hair clashing cheerfully with her lavender dress. Bryan had met her at the rehearsal last night. A resident of Birmingham, Alabama, she had a slow drawl and a quick sense of humor. He followed Angie's progress down the aisle, and watched as she took her assigned place at the front of the church, opposite Jason.

When he glanced back down the aisle, he had the sensation of being kicked solidly in the chest.

Grace was coming toward him, her steps measured and timed to the music, her long, lavender dress fluttering prettily around her. She wore her hair up, baring her slender neck and shoulders, and she carried a small bouquet of white roses in front of her.

She looked so beautiful it made him ache.

He had the feeling she was deliberately not looking at him as she came up the aisle; she seemed to be focusing rather intently on the altar straight ahead of her. He couldn't take his eyes off her.

He was struck by the utter rightness of this moment—waiting for her at the front of a church.

What, exactly, did that mean?

Still without looking at him, Grace took her place. The organ music swelled and the audience rose to their feet as Chloe entered on the arm of her father. Bryan glanced that way, noted that Chloe did, indeed, look beautiful—and then his eyes turned back to Grace.

Maybe she felt his attention on her. Or maybe it was only happenstance that she finally looked his way. Their eyes met, and held for so long that others must have noticed. But this was no act. It wasn't romantic posturing for the sake of anyone who might be watching them. They looked at each other because they couldn't look away—at least, he couldn't.

The ceremony proceeded, and Bryan and Grace managed to perform their responsibilities as best man and maid of honor. Bryan got a lump in his throat when the minister pronounced Donovan and Chloe husband and wife. He swallowed, then broke into a big grin when Donovan kissed his bride. Grace, he noted, had a sheen of tears in her eyes, but he knew her too well to think she would let them escape.

He still remembered the day less than a year earlier when he had confided in Donovan that he wanted to marry and start a family. Donovan had listened to Bryan's carefully thought-out plan for finding the ideal bride and then had said it sounded to him like a disaster waiting to happen. He hadn't understood why Bryan was in such a hurry to get married or to have kids. As far as Donovan was concerned, he and Bryan were both better off being free of marital responsibilities, able to concentrate on business, to travel at will, and to spend their time doing exactly what they wanted without worrying about checking in with anyone else.

Who would have believed then that only a few months later it would be Donovan taking marriage vows while Bryan, still single, looked on?

Donovan and Chloe turned to walk back down the aisle together. Bryan stepped up behind them, offering his arm to Grace, while Jason and Angie fell into step behind them. He doubted that anyone else noticed Grace's momentary hesitation before she rested her hand lightly on his arm. She was avoiding his eyes again. He leaned over to murmur in her ear, "You look stunning."

"Thank you," she whispered.

"Think we could bribe the minister to perform another ceremony? I'm game if you are."

Her steps faltered a moment. Through a frozen

smile, she hissed at him, "That isn't funny. Behave yourself."

He wondered what she would say if he told her that he wasn't entirely sure he'd been teasing.

Grace never expected that Bryan would be a lifeline she would cling to during the wedding reception. She had planned to avoid him as much as possible while still carrying on the pretense that they were a happy couple. But as the evening wore on, she found herself using him more and more as a buffer between her and everyone else.

Bryan was so good at this socializing thing. He knew exactly what to say in response to even the most trivial small talk. He was particularly adept at diverting questions he didn't want to answer without offending the asker. Grace envied his tact and forbearance; she could have used a little of it herself.

She had developed a strategy of her own for coping with too-personal remarks. Every time someone asked about her plans for the future, she smiled, took a sip of champagne and let Bryan field the question. She did that a lot during the course of the reception. Might as well make use of his talents for this one last big event, she rationalized.

"The band is very good," Bryan commented to Chloe and Donovan after the cake had been cut and the first dance was behind them.

Chloe nodded in satisfaction. "They are, aren't they? The lead singer is an old friend from Searcy. The band's getting quite popular locally. I was lucky to get them tonight."

Bryan listened for another minute, his foot tapping

in time to the beat, and then he asked, "Do they have aspirations of going national?"

Donovan gave Grace a wry smile. "Apparently he's considering getting into the music production business now."

"I was just wondering," Bryan answered mildly, his attention still focused on the talented musicians.

Chloe turned to put a hand on her sister's arm. "Grace—you will sing for me tonight, won't you? You promised you would, you know."

Grace took another quick gulp of champagne. "Um…"

Her twin smiled, not without sympathy. "Don't try to weasel out of it now. I know you and the band have practiced and I'm holding you to your promise. For me."

For Chloe. "Of course," Grace replied. "I'll sing. For you."

Having overheard her, Bryan turned to look at her in surprise. "You're going to sing?"

"Grace has a beautiful voice," Chloe informed him proudly. "I sing well enough, but she got the real talent in the family. It's just rare that anyone can talk her into using it."

Self-conscious now, Grace shrugged. "Chloe has always overstated my talent."

"She promised to sing my two favorite songs," Chloe said, leaning happily against Donovan's arm. "I begged, of course. Shamelessly."

"And, as usual, Grace consented as a favor to you," Bryan murmured.

Both Chloe and Grace looked at him in question at his tone. Donovan frowned at his friend, apparently also hearing something that bothered him.

"Bryan, you make it sound as though everything Grace does is for me," Chloe said a bit hesitantly. "I certainly don't—"

"Bryan is well aware that I do exactly what I want to do," Grace cut in, giving him a stern look that dared him to say anything to upset her sister this evening.

"And tonight you want to sing for your sister's wedding?" he asked, his tone hard to read.

She lifted her chin. "Exactly."

With a wry expression, he motioned toward the stage.

Draining her champagne, she set the empty flute on a table and moved toward the band, her long skirt swishing around her ankles. Seeing her approaching, the lead singer, after finishing the number he'd been singing, motioned for her to join them.

"As a special gift for the newlyweds, the bride's sister would like to sing two of the bride's favorite songs," he announced into the microphone. The statement was greeted by murmurs of pleasure and anticipation from the guests, who immediately gathered around the stage, led by the twins' proud parents.

Grace wasn't usually nervous when she sang. She'd been singing in public since her Bible School debut when she was four. She'd sung for big crowds and small groups, for close friends and total strangers— but she had never performed in front of Bryan before. That made it different.

She looked at Chloe as she began. Her twin appeared so delighted that it encouraged Grace to put everything she had into the performance. Standing on the stage in the dress her sister had selected for her, she sang the songs her sister loved. "Someone to

Watch Over Me''—which was particularly appropriate since Donovan had been serving as Chloe's bodyguard when they'd fallen in love—and ''Can You Feel the Love Tonight.''

It was sometime during the first song that Chloe stopped watching Grace and turned her eyes to her new husband's face. He smiled down at her, and their eyes locked. Grace finished the second number with a wistful ache in her chest.

Her audience erupted into enthusiastic applause when she finished. Giving them a little bow of gratitude, she handed the microphone back to the band's lead singer and moved to the three steps that led down from the stage.

Bryan was there to take her hand and assist her down the steps, even though she could, of course, have handled them on her own. He leaned over to kiss her lightly when she stood beside him. Because she knew that would be expected of them, she didn't try to resist the kiss, though she didn't exactly respond, either.

''Chloe didn't overstate your talent,'' he said. ''You have a beautiful voice. Absolutely beautiful.''

As talented an actor as Bryan was, Grace had learned to tell when he was being sincere. He was now. Because that sincerity touched her, she smiled up at him. ''Thank you.''

He squeezed her hand, then moved to stand just behind her while she accepted hugs from her sister and her parents and glowing compliments from the others there.

The approval was nice, of course, but it quickly became overwhelming. Somehow Bryan knew the exact moment when it became too much for her. He moved to her side and slipped an arm around her. "You must be thirsty after singing, darling. Would you like another glass of champagne?"

She gave him a grateful nod. "Yes, I would. I'll go with you to get it."

As always, the crowd parted to allow him through.

"You really do come in handy occasionally," Grace told him as she accepted a glass from him.

He lifted his own in a mock toast. "Just keep that in mind, okay?"

She sipped the champagne rather than attempting to answer him.

"We haven't danced yet," he reminded her as the band began to play again.

She was aware of that. She'd rather hoped to avoid it, even though she'd known the chances of doing so were slim. People would expect to see her dancing with Bryan. And they did dance well together. The problem was, she enjoyed it entirely too much.

She downed several more swallows of champagne before Bryan gently removed the glass from her hand and set it aside. "I think you've had enough of this for now. Come dance with me, Grace."

She just hated it when he spoke in that particular tone. That low, sexy, intimate growl that made her knees go weak and her stomach all quivery. Really hated it, she thought as she moved into his arms.

You are such a liar, Grace.

Chapter Thirteen

"Chloe looked so beautiful tonight." Grace sniffled a little as she made the pronouncement, her voice muffled by the two bouquets she held to her face.

"She was spectacular. Watch your skirt."

Obligingly lifting her long lavender skirt, she stepped out of the elevator. "That was so sweet when Donovan kissed her just before he helped her into the car while everyone threw birdseed at them."

"I'm surprised they weren't attacked by a flock of hungry sparrows. Where's your key?"

"Hmm? Oh, it's in my purse. Somewhere. I can't believe my sister is married. Chloe Chance—that sounds a little strange, doesn't it?"

He dug into the tiny beaded bag she had carried to the wedding. "So she is taking Donovan's name?"

"Oh, sure. Chloe's very traditional about things like that. Wasn't she beautiful?"

Chuckling a little, he unlocked her door and opened it for her. "Almost as beautiful as her sister."

"Mmm. She threw the bouquet right at me, you know. I had to catch it or get clobbered by it. Really made Angie mad—she was hoping to catch it."

Ushering her inside, Bryan closed the door behind them. "Why don't you sit down while I make some coffee?"

"I've got to get out of these shoes."

Taking the bouquets, he moved toward the kitchen. "I'll put these in the refrigerator so they'll stay fresh. You take off your shoes and get comfortable."

"Thank you," she said very politely, sinking onto her couch.

His mouth twisting, he answered gravely, "You're welcome."

After stashing the flowers, he rummaged for coffee and filters. It was a bit late for coffee, but Grace had sipped quite a bit of champagne during the reception. He understood what had made her do so. She'd been uncomfortable in her role as maid of honor, in addition to the continued part as his lover. And it had been an emotional day for her.

Chloe and Donovan weren't the only ones whose lives had been changed by their wedding, he mused. Grace had been accustomed to doing things with her twin, having Chloe as her best friend as well as her sister. Now they didn't even share the same last name. While their feelings for each other hadn't changed, their relationship would never be quite the same. Bryan had seen the wistfulness in Grace's expression when she'd watched Donovan's car drive away from the reception.

He'd been aware of similar feelings, himself. Donovan had been his best friend since high school. They'd been through a lot together, raised some hell together, built Bryan Falcon Enterprises together. Bryan had been accustomed to having Donovan available to him at a moment's notice. Having Donovan's first loyalty be to him. That, too, had changed tonight.

"Bryan?" Grace called from the other room.

He stepped to the doorway. She was sitting on the couch, her bare feet propped on the coffee table, her hair disheveled around her face. Apparently she had pulled the pins out, giving her a rumpled, just-out-of-bed look that made him have to clear his throat before he asked, "What is it?"

She frowned as though trying to remember. And then she nodded. "I just wanted to tell you there's a plate of brownies on the counter if you're hungry. They're covered with aluminum foil. I made them myself—with pecans."

"Sounds good. I'll bring us both some."

"Okay. You want me to make some coffee?"

He grinned. "I've got it covered. You just sit tight."

"Okay." She sighed and wiggled her bare toes.

Torn between laughing and groaning, Bryan turned back to the kitchen, and reminded himself that a true gentleman would never take advantage of a woman who'd had too much champagne.

He knew Grace drank her coffee black. He balanced two filled mugs and the plate of brownies when he rejoined her in the other room.

"You're pretty good at that. Don't tell me you ever worked as a waiter," she said, reaching out to help him set the things on the coffee table.

"Actually I did. The summer I was sixteen, I took

a job at a pizza parlor because a girl I had a crush on worked there—and because it ticked my father off that a Falcon was schlepping pizza. He made me quit after a few weeks. To be honest, I was relieved. I hated the job and I had discovered that the girl had the most annoying giggle I'd ever heard. Drove me nuts."

Grace laughed, and he thought of how different it was with her. He loved hearing her laugh. He would like to hear it more often.

Sitting on the couch beside her, he placed a coffee mug in her hands. "Drink," he ordered. "But be careful, it's hot."

"I'm not really intoxicated, you know," she murmured into the mug. "Just a little buzzy."

"I know. But drink the coffee, anyway." He bit into a brownie. "This is great. You're a good cook."

Leaning close to him, she lowered her voice to a conspiratorial whisper. "I used a mix. All I did extra was throw in a handful of chopped pecans."

"They're still good." He finished the brownie and washed it down with a couple of sips of coffee. And then he set the cup on the table and leaned back, draping an arm casually across the back of the couch. "Long day, wasn't it? That best man gig was more exhausting than I expected."

She gave him a companionable pat on the knee. "You did it very well. And your toast was great. I'm particularly pleased—for my sake and for Chloe's—that you were able to announce that Wallace Childers was captured in Texas and will be brought to justice for his part in Chloe's kidnapping."

Apparently the coffee hadn't kicked in yet. She was still entirely too friendly to him. While he enjoyed it, he'd like to believe her affability was generated by more than champagne. Maybe food would help.

He reached for another brownie, broke off a corner and held it to her lips. "I thought you would like that. It definitely means we can ease off on the security a little. Not entirely, of course, since some crackpot could still try to emulate his scheme, but that's unlikely. Here," he added before she could attempt to argue that she no longer needed any sort of security. "Try some. It really is good. And you didn't eat anything at the reception."

"I was too nervous," she admitted before taking the tidbit he offered her.

As a result of the feel of her lips against his fingertips, he had to clear his throat again before he asked, "Why were you nervous?"

She swallowed, then replied, "Lots of reasons. I was afraid I would trip over this stupid long skirt and fall flat on my face. I worried about saying something stupid and embarrassing Chloe on her wedding day. I knew she wanted me to sing, and I was a little concerned about forgetting the words, since I didn't know the songs very well."

"You never told me you had such a beautiful voice."

She arched an eyebrow over the rim of her coffee mug. "The subject never came up."

"I loved hearing you sing. You were wonderful."

"Thanks. But, um, how much champagne did *you* have?"

He smiled. "The champagne had nothing to do with my appreciation of your voice. Have you ever performed professionally?"

"Thinking of signing me as the second client for your music production company?"

"Donovan was only joking about that. He knows I'm not really interested in starting a music production company."

"All that hobnobbing in Hollywood, and you aren't interested in investing in the entertainment business?"

"I'll stick with science and technology investments for now. You didn't answer my question. Have you ever considered performing professionally?"

She shrugged and looked away from him. "I'm sure every young girl dreams at some point of being a famous singer. I did my share of posturing in front of my bedroom mirror with a hairbrush for my microphone. But I grew up."

"You seemed to enjoy singing at the reception."

"I like to sing occasionally," she agreed offhandedly, setting her cup on the table beside his. "Not necessarily the songs Chloe selected, of course."

"Oh?" He broke off another bite of the brownie and held it to her lips. "What type of songs do you prefer?"

Distracted by the conversation, she took the brownie. Again there was that pleasant frisson of sensation when her lips moved against his fingers. He watched her swallow before she answered vaguely, "A little of this, a little of that. Do you sing?"

"Teenage boys don't perform with hairbrushes. We stood in the shower with a bar of soap pretending to be rock stars. In high school choir, I sang tenor—got a standing ovation for 'Danny Boy.'"

She had tensed a bit when he'd pressed her about her singing. He was glad to see that his self-mockery relaxed her again. "I bet that was something," she murmured.

"I made musical history." He brushed a strand of hair away from her face, letting his fingers linger to stroke her cheek. "I hope you'll sing for me again sometime."

A wave of pink stained the delicate skin he touched. "Well...you never know," she murmured. "Um, do you want some more coffee or...or something?"

His fingers were tangled in her hair now, his other hand rising to her cheek. "I definitely want something," he said, his mouth close to hers. "But not coffee."

He heard her breath catch. Wide and wary, her eyes met his. He was glad to see that they were clear, no longer clouded by champagne or residual wedding sentimentality. She knew exactly what he meant, and she was fully aware of what was happening—or could very easily happen—between them. She knew, as well, that he was leaving the next move up to her. He sat very still, their gazes locked, his mouth an inch above hers, just waiting for her signal. Would she pull him closer, or push him away?

He groaned in satisfaction when she lifted her mouth to his.

Grace wasn't thinking entirely clearly, but she couldn't blame it on the champagne. The effects of that had mostly worn off now. This lapse was due entirely to having Bryan's arms around her, his mouth on hers.

Common sense told her to put a stop to this right now, to pull herself out of his arms and send him on his way before things got out of hand. And she would do just that, she promised herself. In a minute.

Her fingers slid into his thick, black hair. He kissed her until she could hardly breathe, and then he turned his attention to other parts of her, kissing her temple, her cheek, the hollow behind her ear, and then trailing his lips down her neck to her bare shoulder.

He lightly nipped the skin there and she shivered. He was so very good at this.

He kissed the hollow of her throat, where her pulse raced so rapidly that he couldn't possibly have misinterpreted her excitement. She knew it would be a waste of energy to pretend she wasn't attracted to him, or that she didn't respond to his kisses and touches. Only a fool would have believed her willpower wasn't very shaky when it came to him—and Bryan Falcon was no fool.

Emotions that had been simmering inside her for hours erupted to the surface, melting her control. All day she had been entirely too aware of Bryan. She had felt his eyes on her as she'd walked up the aisle ahead of her sister, and all during the ceremony. He'd watched her as she sang at the reception and as she mingled with the other guests. And when they had danced, he'd held her within the bounds of propriety, but close enough to remind her how it felt to be pressed fully against him.

It felt fabulous.

His mouth was on hers again, moving more urgently this time. His hands raced over her, stimulating every nerve ending, leaving her quivering and aching for more.

They weren't in his car this time. No one was watching them, and there was little chance of anyone interrupting them. Bryan was making his feelings clear about how he would like the evening to end. It was up to her to decide if she wanted to spend the rest of the night alone.

Her hands cupping his face, she drew back to look at him. His face was a bit flushed, his dark hair tumbled from her hands, his eyes glittering and heavy-lidded. She felt the tension in him, the faint quiver of muscles held tightly under control. She was sprawled half across his lap, and the hardness against her thigh told her how strongly he, too, had been affected by their kisses.

There was no doubt in her mind that he wanted her, at least for tonight. And there was no question that she wanted him, either—or that she had wanted him for longer than she cared to admit.

She wasn't sure she had the strength to send him away this time. Not tonight. But if she was very careful, she should be able to give into impulse just this once without having her life forever changed or her heart broken. It was simply a matter of keeping in mind that she and Bryan were together for only a little while. That there was no future for them. Only tonight.

Tonight would have to be enough.

Still framing his face in her hands, she leaned forward to kiss him lightly. "Have I ever shown you the rest of my apartment?" she asked.

"No." His voice was husky. "I don't believe you have."

"There's not much," she said, dropping another kiss on his firm chin. "Only a small bedroom. But the bed is big enough for two."

Emotion flared in his eyes, but he remained still, speaking doubtfully. "You're asking me to stay?"

"Yes. If you want to."

"I think you know the answer to that."

"Then stay," she said simply.

"We need to talk."

She kissed him again, letting her tongue sweep his lips and her breasts rest against him. "We've talked enough tonight," she murmured against his mouth.

His arms tightened spasmodically around her. "I hope this isn't the champagne speaking."

"It's not the champagne," she assured him, wriggling out of his arms. She rose and held out her hand to him. "Let me show you my bedroom, Bryan."

Holding her gaze with his, he rose very slowly and took her hand.

Grace soon found out that her imagination had been woefully inadequate when it came to making love with Bryan. She had known he would look gorgeous beneath his clothes, but actually seeing him without his shirt made her breath lodge hard in her throat. Running her hands over his smooth, sleekly muscled chest, she reveled in his warmth. He still wore a small bandage on his left forearm, mostly, she suspected, to protect the raw skin from rubbing against his clothes. Even that looked enticing on him.

She placed her mouth against his throat, nibbling a line of kisses from his jaw to his shoulder and down to his firm, flat nipple. She felt the rapid rhythm of his pulse, and heard the increase in his breathing, and she smiled. It was nice to know she could affect him with her touch—after all, turnabout was fair play.

His hands moved behind her, and she felt cool air on her back as her long zipper parted. Moments later, the dress fell to her feet in a swath of glittery lavender fabric. She stepped out of it, leaving her clad only in a tiny strapless bra and a mere triangle of lace panties.

She'd bought the sexy undergarments only the day before, even though she'd had other, more practical choices that would have sufficed. She supposed she'd suspected even then that Bryan might be seeing them.

She was glad now that she'd gone to the extra effort. Bryan's eyes all but glazed over when he stepped back to look at her. Talk about a boost to her ego...

He moved quickly. One minute she was standing in front of him, and the next she was lying beneath him on her bed.

Her breathless laugh was smothered beneath his mouth. Her arms went around him and her bare legs tangled with his still-clothed ones. She was going to have to get those tuxedo pants off him—in a minute, she thought as she arched into his roaming hands.

Scraps of lace flew, baring her completely to his leisurely exploration. She couldn't be still as he touched her with his fingertips, his lips, the tip of his tongue, and the edge of his teeth. She had to touch him, to move against him, to press her lips against whatever part of him she could reach.

Her hands finally found the fastenings of his pants. Bryan cooperated as she unsnapped them, and then the pants joined her clothes on the bedroom floor. When his underwear followed, she thought she might very well hyperventilate.

She'd known from that first day Bryan had strolled into her shop that she'd never met a man like this before. She'd been aware even then that he could be dangerous.

But this was no time for fear, and too late for hesitation. She pushed her doubts to the back of her mind and melted into him.

Passion flowed between them, so hot she wouldn't have been surprised if steam rose from their damp bodies. Their breathing was labored, their movements frantic.

Grace had never seen Bryan when he wasn't in complete control—not even when he lost his temper. He wasn't in control now. While his actions were still skillful enough to drive her to the point of insanity, there was nothing calculated or premeditated about them.

For once, they weren't putting on an act or performing for an audience or following a predetermined plan. They were just Bryan and Grace, letting instinct and emotion guide them.

Nothing had ever felt more right to her.

By the time he finally donned protection and came back to her, she thought she might just explode if they didn't finish this soon. She pulled him to her with eager hands, her mouth fusing with his as he settled between her invitingly upraised knees.

They fit perfectly together—but she shouldn't read too much into that, she reminded herself, trying to retain a modicum of perspective even at that emotional moment. And then she couldn't think at all. Didn't even try.

She would have plenty of time to think later.

"Grace," he gasped, stiffening against her.

Just hearing her name on his lips sent her over the edge. She was unable to speak coherently enough to say his name in return, but it echoed in her mind as she floated on waves of sensation.

Bryan was the first to be able to move again,

though she couldn't have said how much time had passed before he did so. With a slight groan, he shifted to roll onto his back beside her, relieving her of his weight. She wouldn't have minded if he'd stayed awhile longer.

Scooping her against him with his right arm, he settled her into his shoulder, his other hand stroking her side, soothing her as she tried to steady her pulse and her breathing. "Are you okay?" he asked, his voice a rough growl.

"I'm fine," she managed to say, though her tongue still felt thick and unresponsive. "Your arm?"

It seemed to take him a moment to understand the question, and then he replied, "Feels great. Just like the rest of me."

She didn't quite believe that he felt no discomfort at all after using his arm so strenuously, but she wouldn't press him about it. She supposed he would tell her if he'd done any lasting damage. Maybe.

The extremely eventful day seemed to be catching up with her. She was suddenly so tired she could barely hold her eyes open. A yawn escaped her before she could stop it.

Bryan laughed softly and dropped a kiss on her temple. "I'll be right back," he murmured. "Don't feel obligated to stay awake for my benefit."

"Mmm." She snuggled her face into the pillow when he slid out from beneath her.

She felt him return to the bed a short while later, but she didn't rouse enough to try to speak to him. She needed to escape into sleep just then—away from the emotions left over from her sister's wedding and from the tumultuous passion she had just shared with Bryan.

She could handle everything, she assured herself. She could move on with her life, get back to the way things had been, emerge unscathed from the events of the past few weeks.

But first she needed some rest. She fell asleep with her cheek on his shoulder and his arms around her. *Just this one night,* was her last coherent thought before blessed oblivion claimed her.

Even still half-asleep, Grace sensed that there was a reason she didn't want to open her eyes Sunday morning. She burrowed deeper into the covers, trying to cling to sleep a little while longer, but something felt wrong. She always slept in an oversized T-shirt and panties, never naked. She wasn't wearing a stitch now.

With a low moan, she finally opened her eyes, squinting against the sunlight filtering through the curtains. She was alone in her bed, thank goodness. She hadn't heard Bryan leave, but he must have slipped out sometime during the night. Whether it was to give her some privacy this morning, or because he hadn't wanted to be stranded here today with nothing to wear but a rumpled tuxedo, she couldn't have said, but she was glad she didn't have to face him just yet.

It chagrined her to realize that her bed felt suddenly big and empty without him in it. After only one night. It was just as well that there wouldn't be any more.

She didn't bother berating herself for her actions last night. She thought of that decision with a sense of inevitability. They had been moving toward that step ever since she had agreed to pose temporarily as his love interest. Call it curiosity or propinquity or a monumental lapse in judgment, but she had known it would happen eventually. Just as she'd known that once they had satisfied their curiosity—or whatever it was—they would have to move on in separate directions.

She didn't spend a long time brushing her teeth, showering or pulling her damp hair into a low ponytail, but she didn't waste a minute. She used that time to pull her composure together, lecture herself about keeping her feelings under control, and rehearse the things she would say next time she spoke to Bryan.

She would be calm, collected and courteous as she explained to him that last night had been very nice, but it wasn't going to happen again. Their lives were too different—*they* were too different—to maintain even a casual relationship. And as for anything else—that was entirely out of the question.

Not that she really believed he was considering anything permanent. She knew about that infamous list of his, and she was well aware that she met very few of his qualifications for a mate.

Dressed in a short T-shirt and low-slung jeans, her feet bare, she headed for the kitchen.

The sight of Bryan standing in the sunlight streaming through the window over her kitchen sink drove most of her carefully practiced words from her mind. The sizzling smile he gave her effectively erased the rest of them.

Chapter Fourteen

"I brought breakfast," Bryan said, motioning toward a fragrant-smelling bakery bag on the table. "And I just started the coffee."

She cleared her throat. "I thought you'd left."

"I did for a while. Ran home and showered and changed," he said, motioning toward his polo shirt and jeans. He'd left the bandage off this time, and while she could still see the reddened, burned areas on his forearm, they already looked much better than they had the last time she'd seen them.

She moved toward the cabinet where she stored coffee mugs, pulling two of them out to give herself something to do while she reminded herself of all the sensible things she'd intended to say to him. She only hoped she didn't forget them again, she thought as he advanced on her with a gleam in his eyes.

"Do you realize that you haven't even given me a

smile yet—much less a good-morning kiss?'' he asked.

She smoothed her hands down her jeans. "I, uh..."

He leaned over to plant a firm kiss on her mouth. "Now how about the smile?" he asked when he drew away.

She gave him a quick, stiff smile in response. "That bag smells delicious," she said, seizing on the first innocuous topic that came to her mind. "What did you bring us?"

He dropped his hands on her shoulders to hold her in place when she would have moved toward the table. "Grace, I know you're a little nervous—that awkward morning-after thing, and all."

"You're right. It is a bit awkward. Maybe we should just have breakfast."

"Fine. We can talk while we eat."

"Talk?" She drew a deep breath. "Maybe we should wait a few days before we get into a serious discussion. You know, just to regain some perspective after the wedding and...and everything."

He shook his head. "Has anyone ever told you that it's very difficult to pin you down for a serious talk? One way or another, you've been putting me off for days."

"We'll have plenty of time to talk later."

He didn't release her shoulders. "When, Grace? Starting tomorrow, you're going to use work for your excuse. Chloe will be away on her honeymoon for a couple of weeks and you're going to have more responsibility at the shop. You're going to tell me you're much too busy and distracted then for a serious talk."

Because she suspected she would have done exactly that for the next two weeks while Chloe was away on her honeymoon, Grace scowled. "I do have responsibilities at work, you know. I don't have whole teams of people to handle details for me. Maybe our little shop isn't as impressive as your business empire, but Chloe and I have bills to pay, and so do our few employees."

That made him frown. "I never said your work wasn't important. I know you'll be very busy for the next couple of weeks, which is one reason I thought we should talk today, while we have the chance."

She pulled away from him. "I really don't see what we have to talk about, anyway. We've accomplished everything we set out to do. Your plan worked great. The wedding went off beautifully and with very little media attention since there was no juicy best-friend-betrayed angle to keep the tabloids interested. You and I had a nice little celebration of our success, and now it's time to wind it down."

She turned to pour herself a cup of coffee, speaking with her back to him. "Seems to me like the only thing left to talk about is how many more public appearances we need to make before we can quietly drift apart. Maybe if you start dating another cute little starlet in a few weeks, everyone will naturally assume you've lost interest in me and moved on to more interesting pursuits."

Bryan had remained quiet while she made that extremely painful little speech. "Are you finished?" he asked when she paused to take a bracing sip of caffeine. He spoke very quietly, no expression at all in his voice.

She set her cup down and braced herself on the counter with both hands. "I'm finished."

"Good. Because that was the biggest load of garbage I've heard in longer than I can remember."

Stung, she swung around to glare at him. "What?"

"You're right, the 'plan' worked great. I'm glad we were able to take some of the pressure off Chloe and Donovan. The wedding was beautiful, they're married now, and I'm sure they will live happily ever after. But to be quite honest, I'm not really interested in discussing their future right now. I'm much more concerned with ours."

She shrugged. "We already know our future. I just described it."

"I've already told you what I thought of your description. Garbage."

She opened her mouth to respond, but he surged on before she had a chance to speak. "Last night was *not* a casual celebration of the successful conclusion of a brilliant plan. It was a hell of a lot more than that, and it's been building for a long time."

"I..."

He didn't give her a chance to finish—which was just as well, because she hadn't a clue what she would have said.

Looming over her, he continued in clipped tones, "As for your clever suggestion that I take up with some 'cute little starlet'—that's not even worth the breath it would take me to respond. Concerning the rest of your comments, I see no need for us to have any more public outings just for the sake of the media. We've put that gossip to rest and everyone has moved on to more juicy speculation."

"Oh. Well, then." If he really thought there was no need for further outings, then they could just end it now. It would be a great relief, she assured herself, not to have to deal with any more high-society events—wondering what to wear, how to do her hair and makeup, what to say, or *not* to say. If she never heard another bored photographer call her name for a fake smile, she wouldn't be at all disappointed. All in all, it would be best to just call it quits right now.

She could deal with the aching hollow left inside her later. She would certainly have plenty of free time to do so once her fake relationship with Bryan was over.

"From now on," Bryan added, "you and I will be together for no other reason than that we want to be. The media will have nothing to do with it."

A dull pounding began somewhere in the back of Grace's skull. So it wasn't going to be as easy as she had hoped to break this off between them. And this was exactly why she had kept putting this talk off. Now she realized she should have made her intentions clear several days ago, before she'd given in to temptation and made love with him last night.

It wasn't going to be easy to convince him that she wasn't interested in him when she had been all over him last night. And especially since she knew very well that she was head over heels in love with him— and probably had been from the first time he had walked into her shop. But that was something she could not allow him to see, since loving him did not make her right for him.

She chose her words carefully. "I'm sure we'll see each other through Chloe and Donovan. Chloe enjoys entertaining, and we'll be invited to dinner parties and that sort of thing."

He was shaking his head long before she finished

speaking. "I'm talking about *us,* Grace. You and me."

"There is no us, Bryan. It was all an act. Don't start confusing that with reality."

His eyes narrowed. "Last night was no act."

"Last night was…" She almost called it a mistake. She bit that word back because she didn't really think of it that way. Maybe it had complicated things between them, but she had no regrets. She was going to savor those memories for a very long time.

"Last night was a one-time thing," she said instead.

"You really think so?" he asked, his voice silky.

She lifted her chin. "I know so."

"I'm wondering which of us is really denying reality now?"

She sighed and planted her fists on her hips. "Just what is it you want from me, Bryan?"

"I want you to marry me."

Grace sagged for a moment against the kitchen countertop, needing its support. Of all the answers she had expected to her exasperated question, a proposal had not been one of them.

"Have you lost your mind?" she asked in a gasp.

Bryan pushed a hand through his hair. "Not exactly the reaction I was hoping for."

"Then let's just pretend you never said what you just said."

"I'm tired of pretending, Grace. This is real."

Taking a few steps away from him, she shook her head. "I think you should leave now. It's obvious that we need some time apart—just to clear our minds and to put some distance between us."

He watched her without making any move to follow her. "You think my mind is clouded?"

She took another few steps away from him. "I think you've gotten carried away by everything that's been going on lately. You know, spending so much time together. You getting hurt. Dinner with your parents. The wedding. And, uh, well—after the wedding."

He crossed his arms over his chest, an odd half smile playing around his lips. "Grace?"

Now she was really getting nervous. Why the hell was he smiling? "What?"

"Where are you going?"

She realized that she had inched so far away from him she was almost entirely out of the kitchen. Embarrassed, she stopped and lifted her chin. "I'm not going anywhere. You are."

"I know you're afraid..."

Her shoulders squaring, she drew herself taller. "I am not afraid of you."

"You're afraid of how you feel about me. I understand. It's safer to protect yourself. To follow your predictable routines, keeping your parents and your sister happy, ignoring your own dreams and wishes."

"You don't know what you're talking about."

"You think I haven't gotten to know you during the past year? Everything you do is for Chloe—making sure she and Donovan got together, going to so much trouble to see that the wedding was unspoiled. Even the shop was Chloe's dream, not yours—but you're the one who'll be doing much of the work there now that she's married."

That stung. She glared at him, almost quivering with temper and suppressed emotion. "And I suppose you consider yourself the well-adjusted one between us? You're the one who went shopping for a wife as though you were looking for a promising new business investment. You're the one who left a string of busty blondes to start tracking down a woman who fit some stupid list of wife requirements because you're such an arrogant control freak you thought you could just order up a wife the way you would a pizza. And then, when it didn't work out with your first choice, you just switched over to her twin sister!''

She had effectively removed the smile from his face. When he moved toward her, she was unable to resist taking another step backward. Not that she was intimidated by his fierce glare, she assured herself. She was simply moving out of his way if he was trying to leave.

He stopped directly in front of her. ''I do *not* consider you to be a convenient substitute for Chloe,'' he said between clenched teeth.

''Don't you?''

''You know damned well I don't. You're using that as an excuse because you're afraid to say what you really want.''

''What I want is for you to leave. *Now,*'' she added, pointing toward the door.

He ignored her gesture. ''I can't believe you would imply that I would ask you to marry me just because Chloe chose Donovan. Do you really think I'm that shallow and…and idiotic?''

He was so mad he was shaking, she realized in amazement. As much as they had been through the past few months, she had never seen him reduced to stammering. ''I don't think you're shallow and idiotic. I think you've just gotten carried away. Everything's been so hectic and Donovan is so happy with Chloe—''

Bryan held up a hand. "You are right about one thing," he cut in. "We need some time to calm down and get our tempers back under control. I'm going to leave now. I want you to do some hard thinking about the time you and I have spent together. And I want you to remember that I have *never* confused you with Chloe."

"Just go," she whispered, horrified at the possibility that she might cry in front of him. "Please."

"I'll go. But I will be back."

It sounded more like a threat than a promise. Expecting him to walk out then, she was caught by surprise when he stopped in front of her, leaned down and planted a hard kiss on her slightly parted lips. "I *will* be back," he said again, staring into her eyes for a moment.

And then he was gone, leaving Grace alone.

She missed her sister, she thought, sinking to the floor with her face in her hands. She missed all the dreams she had once had. Most of all, she missed Bryan.

As badly as she hurt now, she knew she had done the right thing to send him away. Not even for Bryan could she pretend to be someone she wasn't. She wouldn't repeat the mistake she had made with Kirk, trying to change herself to fit the image he had of the ideal woman. And unless she changed, she would never fit into Bryan's high-profile, socially conscious world. It was a disaster waiting to happen, and she wanted no part of it.

She was sure once Bryan had time to think about how different she was from the woman he had hoped to marry, he would agree that she'd been right to send him away.

But, oh, it hurt—as nothing had ever hurt her before.

Bryan couldn't remember the last time he'd been so damned angry. He was known for having a coldly dangerous temper, soft-spoken and effective. Only Grace could push him into yelling.

He tried to spend some time working at home that afternoon, but found himself unable to concentrate. Instead he paced, muttering to himself as he did so. He still couldn't believe Grace had accused him of using her as a substitute for Chloe. He knew she was scared and uncertain about their relationship, but that had been a low blow.

If he thought she truly believed it, he'd *really* be upset.

"Um…boss?" Jason looked up from a folder containing a report of Wallace Childers's capture at the Texas border. "Are you sure you want to discuss this today? You seem a little…agitated."

Bryan whirled to face his security chief. "Am I arrogant? A control freak?"

Jason looked bemused by the questions. "Just how do you want me to answer?"

"Honestly."

Clearing his throat, his subordinate drawled, "Well…if by control freak you mean someone who's sort of obsessed with having everything just the way you want it, someone who likes all his ducks in a row and doesn't leave anything to chance, then yeah, I guess you're a bit of a control freak."

"And arrogant?"

Jason shifted in his chair. "Well…maybe just a tad. Not in a bad way, of course."

"And do you also consider me an idiot?" Bryan demanded.

Jason looked intrigued. "Grace called you an idiot? You must have really hacked her off."

"She didn't actually call me an idiot. She just implied that I am one. Can you believe she accused me of thinking she was interchangeable with her sister? She implied that I'm interested in her now only because Chloe married Donovan."

"Well, aren't you?"

"*No,* damn it!"

Jason tilted his head to one side, obviously intrigued by seeing his employer and friend so agitated. "No, I see that you aren't."

"What kind of man do you people think I am?" Bryan ranted, throwing up his arms as he spun to pace again.

"I take it Grace broke up with you?"

Bryan didn't usually unload his personal problems on his employees, or even his friends, with the exception of Donovan. But Donovan wasn't here, and Bryan needed someone to talk to. "I asked her to marry me."

"Did you?" Jason didn't look particularly surprised.

"She turned me down. She accused me of swapping her for her sister. And she called me an arrogant control freak."

Jason smiled a little. "She does have a temper, that one."

"Yes, she does. Entirely unlike Chloe, who is very slow to anger. Other than their appearance, they're almost nothing alike. I certainly didn't propose to Grace because she reminds me of her sister.''

"Then why *did* you propose to her?'' Jason asked mildly.

That took him aback. Stopping in his tracks, Bryan shoved a hand through his hair. ''Why?''

Leaning back in his chair, Jason laced his hands behind his head. ''Yep. Why did you ask her to marry you?''

"For the usual reasons, of course. I enjoy being with her. I admire and respect her. I think we've very compatible.''

"She fits the list you made up?''

"This has nothing to do with any list,'' Bryan growled. ''This has to do with Grace, and the way I feel about her.''

"And how *do* you feel about her?'' Jason asked patiently.

"I'm in love with her,'' Bryan snapped. And then he repeated it more slowly as the words sank in. ''I'm in love with her.''

"Did you tell her that?''

Grimacing, Bryan shook his head. ''No.''

"What did you tell her?''

"I just told her I wanted to marry her. And that it had nothing to do with Chloe.''

"And you expected her to accept that without question. Even though you made the newspapers less than two years ago for being engaged to that bathing-suit model. And only a few months ago you were talking to Chloe about getting married. Hell, I can't imagine why Grace thought she was just next in line for a proposal, can you?''

Bryan groaned. ''You're fired, Colby.''

Jason chuckled, not without sympathy. "For answering you honestly?"

"For making me realize that I have, indeed, been an idiot."

"I wouldn't say you've been an idiot. A little misdirected when it comes to romance, maybe, but how many men do you know who *aren't* clueless when it comes to that sort of thing? I'm divorced, myself, you know. And it wasn't so long ago that Donovan was swearing he wasn't ever going to get married, and now he's off on his honeymoon. So we *are* capable of changing—with the right incentive."

Bryan sighed. "I've got my work cut out for me, don't I?"

"Oh, yeah. She's going to make you crawl."

Nodding in resignation, Bryan turned toward the door. "I've got to do some thinking. I'll see you later."

"Yeah, sure. Um—you want me to keep going through this report, or should I be looking for another job?"

"Go through the file. You're hired again—until the next time you show me up for the fool I am."

"Nice to have job security," Jason grumbled sarcastically, but Bryan didn't pause to respond.

He had to come up with a whole new plan.

The roses arrived at the shop on Monday. Two dozen of them. They were a vivid yellow, tinged with fuchsia edges, the most unusual roses Grace had seen in a long while.

Nearly hidden by the enormous bouquet, Justin carried them into her office. "Are these delicious, or what?" he demanded, looking rather enviously at the blooms. "They must have cost a fortune. That man sure has a thing for you, Grace."

Because Justin was one of the few people who knew the truth about why Bryan and Grace had been dating, she made a face at him. "He'll get over it," she muttered, watching as he set the vase carefully on Chloe's empty desk. "Just like he did all the others."

"Mmm. I wouldn't be so sure. I've been watching the two of you."

"Go tend to our customers, Justin."

He grinned impertinently and flipped her the envelope that had been tucked among the roses. "Chicken," he murmured as he left the office.

Grace felt decidedly cowardly as she held the small envelope in her hands, working up the courage to open it. When she finally did, she frowned as she read the words.

Chloe prefers pastel roses. These are much more suited to your tastes. Bryan.

He was right, of course. Chloe would have found these colorful roses a bit gaudy. Grace adored them. So what was Bryan trying to prove? That he knew what sort of flowers she liked, just because he'd twice given her roses that she found beautiful?

Hardly a basis for marriage, she thought with a sniff, annoyed with him all over again.

But they really were beautiful, she thought, unable to resist leaning over just to inhale their fragrance.

On Tuesday he sent her a two-pound box of dark chocolates. And she suspected that he was well aware that Chloe didn't like dark chocolates. Chloe preferred milk chocolate, because she thought the dark kind was too rich. As far as Grace was concerned, the darker the better when it came to chocolate.

So Bryan knew her tastes in flowers and candy, she thought, glowering at the beautiful gold box of sweets. So he noticed things like that. Was she supposed to be impressed?

The gift she received Wednesday was harder to brush off.

She carried the wrapped package to her office to open it away from her employees' avidly curious eyes. What would it be this time? Jewels? If so, she was sending them back immediately, she decided with a scowl. Surely Bryan was aware that she couldn't be bought.

Lifting the lid of the small box she had unwrapped, she frowned and lifted out a beautifully carved wooden box. Not just a box, she realized, turning it over. A music box. She wound it up, then opened the lid. Two intricately detailed plastic figures inside began to twirl to the tinkling notes of "Misty."

It was one of the first songs they had danced to together, she remembered. She had almost forgotten. It stunned her that Bryan remembered.

She closed the lid abruptly, stopping the music in mid-note. And then she picked up her phone and dialed his number without having to look it up.

"This has to stop," she said when he answered, not bothering to identify herself. "No more gifts."

"You haven't liked them?"

"That isn't the point, and you know it. It's over, Bryan."

His reply was a silky, "Not by a long shot, darling."

She hung up on him.

She wasn't at all sure what she had accomplished with that terse phone call, but something told her it hadn't been what she'd hoped. Just hearing Bryan's voice again had renewed the dull ache that hadn't completely gone away since she'd all but thrown him out of her apartment last Sunday. And it had been clear from his tone that he had no intention of quietly giving up and going away.

She groaned and buried her face in her hands. Just what had she gotten herself into when she'd agreed to that crazy plan of his? And how was she going to get out of it without having her heart shattered in the process? Or was it already too late for that?

Chapter Fifteen

Grace didn't bother trying to hide her actions as she left her apartment Friday evening, her car keys in her hand. Now that Wallace Childers had been captured and she and Bryan weren't seeing each other, she doubted that he was having her watched as obsessively as he had been before the wedding.

She hadn't seen him since last Sunday. Nor had she received any more gifts from him since she'd called him Wednesday. Maybe he'd finally gotten the message. And maybe she would survive if she never saw him again, but there were times—particularly in the middle of the long, lonely nights—when she doubted it.

She couldn't stand another quiet, solitary evening in her apartment, which was now haunted by his presence, especially in her bedroom. So, she had changed into an off-the-shoulder red sleeveless top and a short black skirt with chunky black sandals, tousled her hair, applied smoky makeup and sparkling jewelry, and headed for the door. There was one place she could always go when she felt trapped or depressed, and she knew she would be welcomed there with open arms and no particular expectations.

It was exactly what she needed tonight.

She parked between two pickup trucks outside a rustic looking establishment on the outskirts of Little Rock. Being a late summer evening, it was still light at nearly 8:00 p.m., but even in the dark she didn't worry about entering this place alone. She spent a lot of time here, and knew she always had an escort if she wanted one. This was where she had come when she'd needed a temporary escape from the stress of pretending to be involved with Bryan, when she'd twice managed to elude his security guards for a few precious hours to herself. Several other patrons were in the parking lot, a few leaving, most just arriving. She nodded to the ones she knew and a few that she didn't. It was that sort of place—impersonally friendly.

Inside, the lights were bright and the noise earsplitting. The décor was a cheerfully chaotic mixture of western and primitive—wooden floors, numerous wall-mounted shelves holding pottery, antique tools and dishes, and a clutter of other curiosa, mirrors framed in ox yokes and barbed wire. Patrons sat on stools at the long bar at the back of the room or at the many tables and booths scattered in the big, open dining space. At the far side of the room was a small stage where a band performed a loud mix of rock oldies and contemporary country hits. Through a big arched opening another room was visible, that one filled with pool tables and pinball machines.

The place was packed on this Friday night, as it usually was on weekends. The clientele here was rowdy, blue collar and proud of it. Grace felt right at home.

Curvaceous young women in tight T-shirts and tighter jeans moved among the tables carrying trays and taking orders. One of them spotted Grace and grinned broadly, her bleached-white hair shining almost blindingly in the overhead lighting. "Hey, Sassy," she called out. "You want a beer?"

"Sure." Grace moved toward the bar, where she smiled at the burly bartender. "Hey, Joe."

"Hey there, beautiful. Glad you could make it tonight. You gonna sing for us?"

"I might. First I want to play some pool."

Joe nodded knowingly. "Stump's back there. You bet he'll take you on."

She smiled and accepted a mug from him. "Thanks. Run a tab for me. I'll go find Stump."

"It ain't like he's easy to miss," Joe called after her, laughing heartily at his own wit.

Stump was definitely hard to miss, Grace mused as she entered the game room where a six-foot-six, three-hundred-pound former linebacker loomed beside a pool table, a cue stick in one ham-sized hand. He wore a faded, camouflage-patterned T-shirt that had shrunk a couple of sizes in the wash, and a pair of jeans that dipped low enough to reveal a bit too much when he leaned over the table to make his shot.

Grace didn't bother to modestly look away. She'd seen that particular view on more than one occasion.

She waited until he'd completed his shot, winning the game, before she spoke. "Hey, Stump."

Having gloated at his soundly defeated opponent, Stump turned with a broad grin splitting his ruddy face. "Hey, Sassy. Ain't you pretty tonight?"

She lifted her face for his smacking kiss. "Thanks, Stump."

"Hey, what's the matter?" He searched her face with eyes that were much more perceptive than his appearance might have implied. "You okay?"

Her lower lip quivered just a little before she could stop it. "I guess you could say I'm suffering from a broken heart tonight. I need some pool, some music, some beer and some friendship to console myself."

She tried to speak lightly, to downplay her pain, but she must not have done a very good job. Stump's eyes narrowed dangerously. "Who's the jerk that hurt you, Sassy? It ain't that wannabe cowboy again, is it?"

She shook her head. "No, I got over Kirk a long time ago. This was someone else. Another foolish mistake on my part."

"Me and Paul will go have a little chat with the jerk, won't we, Paul?"

The skeletally thin cowboy who had just been soundly defeated at pool nodded enthusiastically. "We can take him."

Grace smiled and shook her head. "Never mind. How about a game, instead?"

Taking her hint to drop the subject, Stump shook his head. "You got your heart broken and now you want me to stomp on your pride?"

She reached for Paul's pool cue. "We'll just see whose pride gets stomped, won't we?"

Stump slapped his friend on the back hard enough to rattle Paul's prominent bones. "Rack 'em up, pard. I gotta give this sassy little lady a lesson in humility."

Rolling her eyes in response to the over-the-top drawl, Grace picked up a square of cue chalk and prepared to forget her troubles for just a few hours.

She hadn't realized that trouble had followed close on her heels.

Bryan looked around curiously as he entered the restaurant/bar he'd been directed to by the bodyguard who had been assigned to discreetly follow Grace that evening. Funny. As well as Bryan knew Little Rock, he'd never even known this place was here.

A busty brunette greeted him with a flirty smile. "Well, hello. I haven't seen you here before."

Bryan gave her one of the smiles that rarely failed to achieve the results he wanted. "I haven't been here before. Looks like a fun place."

Raising her voice over the sound of the band, she replied, "It can be, when things really get going. You want a table or are you going to sit at the bar?"

"Actually I'm looking for someone. Grace Pennington. Do you know her?"

The woman frowned a bit and shook her head. "I don't think so. Maybe she isn't here yet?"

According to the employee who had called him, Grace had entered this establishment just over half an hour ago. Bryan shook his head. "I'll just look around for her, if you don't mind."

The woman shrugged. "Help yourself. You can order at the bar, and if you decide you want a table, just give me a sign. There's pool and pinball in the back room if you're in the mood for a game."

''Thanks. I'll check it out.''

She nodded and moved away in response to a summons from a table crowded with three thirty-something couples who looked ready to place their orders. Not wanting to look more conspicuous than he already did in his pressed khakis and neat polo shirt, Bryan moved to the bar, where he ordered a beer from an almost stereotypically jolly bartender and perched on a stool to survey the crowded room. He didn't usually drink domestic beer, but that seemed to be the beverage of choice here. Had he been warned what the place was like, he'd have changed into jeans and boots before coming.

He didn't spot Grace among the diners or the few dancers crowding a postage-stamp-sized dance floor. He couldn't see into the other room from this angle; was it possible that Grace hustled pool in her spare time? At this point, nothing would surprise him.

Carrying his barely touched beer, he made his way across the room to the archway, exchanging a few polite nods on the way. A few women blatantly checked him out, sending him inviting smiles that he pretended not to see. Some of them were old enough to be his mother, others damn near young enough to be his daughter.

Where the hell was Grace?

He spotted her the minute he paused in the game room doorway. She was bent over a pool table, her short skirt just this side of decent as she expertly lined up a difficult shot with her pool cue. Half a dozen men stood around watching her—no surprise, he thought with a scowl. She seemed to be pitting her skills against a man who was roughly the size of a redwood tree—he was even dressed in a foliage-print shirt.

With a sharp crack, her cue ball hit its target, and her audience cheered, sloshing beer and slapping each other on the backs.

"Damn," her oversized opponent growled, shaking his head. And then he grinned and pulled Grace into an enthusiastic one-armed hug that must surely have left a few bruises on her tender skin. "You are one hell of a pool player, Sassy."

Sassy? Wasn't that the name her father had called her when she'd rebelled as a child? Bryan stared at her as she grinned up at the big man who held her. "Thanks, Stump," she said. "But then, you taught me nearly everything I know."

"That I did, kid," he agreed, planting a smacking kiss on her nose before he set her back on her feet.

A man in a black-and-red Western shirt, so thin he almost rattled when he moved, stepped out of the group of watchers. "Play me next, Sassy. I'm tired of getting beat by Stump. It'd be nice to be beat by someone prettier this time."

"Give me a minute to finish my beer, Paul," she replied, reaching for a half-filled mug sitting on a convenient ledge behind her. "Playing Stump always makes me thirsty, for some reason."

Bryan moved swiftly, the mug in his free hand before her fingers closed around it. She turned in question, and her face went pale as her eyes widened almost comically.

"I believe this is yours?" he asked silkily, holding her mug out to her.

"What are you—how did you—you followed me

here, didn't you?'' she sputtered, her face suddenly flooding with vivid color.

''Well, to be accurate, I had you followed. Interesting place. Come here often?''

''Go away,'' she ordered him, more desperation than anger in her voice now.

The huge man who'd hugged her moved close behind her, looking mean enough to intimidate a tank. ''Is this the guy, Sassy? The one who broke your heart?''

Bryan figured there was a very good chance that he was about to die. But he found some solace in the other man's words. ''She told you I broke her heart?''

''What makes you think I was talking about you?'' Grace asked, with a toss of her curled hair.

He smiled. ''Darling, I know you were.''

Stump moved another step closer, and Bryan could have almost sworn he felt the floor tremble just a little beneath his feet. ''Me and the guys here don't like it when people hurt our friends, do we, boys?''

''No, we don't.'' Skinny Paul stood with his feet spread and his arms akimbo on his nonexistent hips, trying to look as fearsome as his large buddy. ''What did he do to you, Sassy?''

''He asked me to marry him,'' she snapped, still glaring at Bryan.

That was obviously not the response they'd been expecting. The men looked at each other and then at Grace. ''Um…?''

''He asked my sister first.''

Half a dozen heads nodded in sudden understanding. ''That was just stupid,'' someone said.

Bryan sighed. ''Yes, I know. I made a mistake, okay? I was looking for the sort of woman who would have been completely and totally wrong for me. I know that now."

"Anybody would be a moron not to want to marry Sassy," an older man with a grizzled beard and a kindly smile offered from the other side of the room. "I've asked her myself about a half dozen times, but she always said no."

"Maybe 'cause you already got a wife, Ernie?" Paul inquired.

The bearded man sighed. "I like to think that's the only reason she turned me down," he acknowledged.

"You don't want to marry me," Grace told Bryan fiercely, her hazel eyes unnaturally bright. "I'm all wrong for you. I don't fit in with your fancy friends and your elegant parties. This is where I'm happiest."

"Then we'll spend a lot of time here and avoid as many of those fancy parties as we can," he assured her, loving her more every minute. "Personally I think you fit in quite nicely wherever you are. I, on the other hand, might have some adjustments to make. Stump, do you know where I can get one of those camo T-shirts?"

"I got mine at Wal-Mart," the big man volunteered.

Paul sighed in disgust. "It was a rhetorical question, Stump. Be quiet and let the man finish begging."

"I *will* beg, you know," Bryan said softly, still holding Grace's gaze with his own. "I've never begged anyone for anything—I've never had to, nor wanted to—but I will this time. Nothing else has ever mattered this much to me."

"I dunno, Grace. I think he's serious," Stump said in a stage whisper. "Did he beg your sister, you think?"

"She knows I didn't," Bryan said flatly, setting both beer mugs on the ledge. "She knows full well that it never got that far between her sister and me—and that it never would have. Chloe and I knew we were wrong for each other even before we finally put it into words. She was in love with my best friend. And I was in love with Grace."

The men looked confused again. Grace nearly choked. "You weren't in love with me!"

"I think I've been in love with you for months," Bryan countered. "But, as both you and my friend Jason pointed out, I was too stupid and arrogant to realize it. And, besides, you said you hated me when we first met, remember?"

"I did hate you—I still do," she added recklessly.

Stump shook his head and patted her on the shoulder, the friendly gesture nearly knocking her off balance. "Now, Sassy, you know you don't mean that. He couldn't have broke your heart if you hated him."

"He has a point there," Bryan suggested hopefully. "Obviously a very intelligent and insightful man."

Stump nodded amenably.

"I love you, Grace," Bryan repeated, moving so close to her that the others would have had to strain to hear his words above the background noises—and most of them seemed to be trying.

He watched her swallow, watched her eyes flood with tears. "I—"

"Sassy, come sing for us," the waitress who'd told Bryan she'd never heard of anyone named Grace Pennington called out from the doorway. "The band's all ready for you."

Grace looked dismayed. "Oh, no, I can't—"

From the other room a chorus of voices called out, "Sassy! Sassy!"

She looked helplessly at Bryan. "I—"

He leaned over to kiss her softly, then drew back. "Sing for us, 'Sassy.' We all want to hear you."

She moistened her lips, then turned and fled.

Grace wondered if there was any chance that she was dreaming. Things like this just didn't happen in her real life.

Had Bryan really followed her here? Had he really just told her he loved her in front of a game room full of men? Had he really said he was willing to beg, if necessary? The thought of Bryan Falcon begging for *anything* was enough in itself to boggle her mind.

She wasn't sure she'd be able to sing a note, but she was almost dragged onto the stage before she could pull herself together enough to protest. She was welcomed warmly by the band—the same ones who had performed at her sister's wedding. Their old school friend, Jack, the lead singer for the increasingly popular band, smiled at her and handed her the microphone. "What do you want to sing, Grace?" he asked, the only one there other than the band members and Bryan who even knew her real name.

"I, uh—" Her mind was blank.

"How about 'Down at the Twist and Shout?'"

"Yes, that will be fine." She cleared her throat and somehow found the mental resources to launch into the rollicking number made famous by country singer Mary Chapin Carpenter.

Bryan was sitting at a table with Stump and Paul now, looking like one of their lifelong pals, which only added to the air of unreality that accompanied her performance. He was grinning and lounging with the ease of a man in his natural environment. Even here, all he had to do was walk in and he had a dozen new best friends, she thought in resignation.

Thundering applause followed the last note of her song, and while she enjoyed the ovation, she was well aware that generous mugs of beer fueled the enthusiasm for her singing. Bryan was on his feet, clapping and whistling and generally making a fool of himself. She sent him a repressive frown and automatically followed along when the band began the next number, Tanya Tucker's "It's a Little Too Late."

This was the music she truly enjoyed singing. Hard rocking, foot tapping contemporary country. She loved bopping with the band, holding the microphone, hearing the audience cheering and clapping along. This was when she flew, free of the restraints of her everyday life. Jack sang backup for her; they leaned toward each other as they harmonized the lyrics about being up all night wondering what to do—and then acknowledging that it was "a little too late" to do the right thing and walk away.

A little too late to turn her heart around, she sang—and realized that the words were absolutely true. It was entirely too late for her to stop loving Bryan. Entirely too late to do the right thing and forget about him.

She'd given him his chance. Now he was stuck with her. And he had better not change his mind this time, she thought as she finished the song and watched him cheer again with his newfound buddies. She couldn't help smiling as Stump slapped him on the back so hard Bryan nearly tumbled flat on his face.

She turned to her friend and whispered into his ear. And then, while he talked to the band, she spoke into the microphone. "I would like to dedicate my final number to someone who's waiting for an answer from me," she said, looking straight at Bryan. "I hope you find it in this song."

The band played the opening notes to a blatantly romantic song made famous by an incongruously violent movie. First recorded by Trisha Yearwood, it was entitled "How Do I Live." The lyrics asked how she could live if the man she loved left her life, taking with him everything that mattered to her. Without him there would be no joy, no sunshine—no love, she crooned.

She had previously considered the song a bit too syrupy, too dramatic. She sang it occasionally only because it had been so often requested by audiences, and because the band liked playing it for her. Now she sang it because she meant it. Maybe she *could* live without Bryan—but she had discovered during the past few days that she really didn't want to.

The applause was a bit more muted when she finished that number—or maybe she had just tuned out everyone but Bryan, who was standing across the room, watching her without taking his eyes from her face. She handed the microphone to Jack and stepped off the stage, murmuring incoherent responses to the compliments she received as she crossed the room.

She stopped in front of Bryan and gazed up at him fiercely. "Well?"

"I can't live without you, either," he said simply. "I love you, Grace."

"I love you, too," she said. "And if you change your mind, I swear I'll...I'll..."

"I'll take care of him for you if that happens," Stump offered, shamelessly eavesdropping.

"There you go," Bryan told her with a grin. "I have no choice but to love you for the rest of my life."

"No," she said, grabbing his shirt and pulling him toward her. "You don't."

She kissed him right there in front of the entire room full of people, sealing the deal.

"Whee-eww," Stump shouted, waving an arm in the air. "Sassy's done got herself engaged. Drinks all around to celebrate—and the rich guy's paying," he added, thumping Bryan on the back.

Bryan seemed delighted to oblige—or maybe he was just scared not to, Grace thought with a happy laugh. She couldn't really blame him.

"Grace?"

Arching into Bryan's lazily stroking hand on her bare, damp back, Grace responded without opening her eyes. She didn't have the energy to do so. "Mmm?"

"How did you find that place, anyway?"

She smiled against his bare chest, her own hand making a leisurely foray down his lean hip. "I used to go there with Kirk—my ex-fiancé. When we broke up, I got custody of the hangout and our friends there. Kirk quit showing up there when Stump threatened to use him for a pool cue."

Bryan chuckled. "Remind me never to get on Stump's bad side."

"No problem. By the time we left tonight, he was ready to marry you, himself."

Laughing, Bryan pulled her more snugly into his

arms, nuzzling her temple. "Why didn't you ever take me there before?"

She opened her eyes to look somberly at him. "I didn't think you would be interested. And I didn't want to face memories of you at the last place in my life you hadn't touched. I thought it would hurt too much when you were gone."

He shook his head. "You had so little faith in me."

"Can you blame me?"

"No," he said with a sigh. "Jason helped me understand why you found it hard to trust me at first. You do believe me now that I never loved Chloe, don't you? I only kissed her a couple of times, and I always had the unsettling feeling that I was kissing a cousin or a sister. It never would have gone any further, no matter what I thought at the time."

"I know. I can't blame you for wanting to love her, though. Chloe is very special."

"Chloe is no more special than you are," he said firmly. "I don't know where you got a different idea, but it's wrong."

She smiled and kissed him. "Thank you. And I do believe you, by the way. I'm not jealous of you and Chloe. I know you never cared about her this way. You never pretended to love her. And you aren't pretending to love me. You really do, heaven help you."

He grinned and settled her comfortably on top of him. "I really do."

She was already making some experimental moves—maybe she had a little energy left, after all—when he spoke again. "Grace?"

Looking up from the nipple she'd been circling with her tongue, she asked distractedly, "Mmm?"

"Do you want to sing? Professionally, I mean, with

a recording contract and everything. Because, if you do…''

"You would arrange it for me," she finished, shaking her head. "I don't want to sing professionally, Bryan. I'm a shopkeeper who likes to sing as an occasional sideline. Maybe I'll sing more now that you've unmasked me, as it were, but I have no desire to tour or spend hours in a recording studio or anything like that—even if I were good enough to make it in that cutthroat business, which I doubt."

He looked as though he would have argued that point, but she didn't give him the chance.

"We'll make our adventures together," she assured him. "I think you're going to find it as challenging to be married to me as I will to be Bryan Falcon's wife. Because I'm not going to change who I am—I couldn't change even if I wanted to. But I think we're up to the test, don't you?"

His hands moved eagerly on her, drawing her back down to him. "I am definitely up to it," he assured her.

She smiled against his lips. Somehow, she thought that old familiar trapped feeling was gone for good now. Bryan's love had freed her. Just as she had freed him from the baggage he had carried from his own past, the fears and insecurities he hadn't realized he had when it came to love.

It was going to be a very interesting ride, she decided happily. And it was going to last a lifetime.

* * * * *

SILHOUETTE®
SPECIAL EDITION™

AVAILABLE FROM 20TH JUNE 2003

BUT NOT FOR ME Annette Broadrick

Rachel Wood had never confessed her love to her boss, millionaire Brad Phillips. So why, when she was in danger, did he insist on whisking her to safety—as his convenient wife?

TWO LITTLE SECRETS Linda Randall Wisdom

After a fortnight in the arms of gorgeous Zachary Stone, Ginna Walker sensed that he had a secret he wasn't ready to share. She was sure that she could handle it...but she didn't know that he had *two* little secrets...

MONTANA LAWMAN Allison Leigh

Montana

Librarian Molly Brewster had a new identity...and Deputy Sheriff Holt Tanner had a case to solve. Would his search for the truth force her into hiding—or would his love set her free and make her his?

NICK ALL NIGHT Cheryl St. John

Shock became passion when sexy single dad Nick Sinclair mistook former neighbour Ryanne Whitaker for an intruder! Could his kisses persuade her to swap city life for the warm glow of hearth and home...forever?

MILLIONAIRE IN DISGUISE Jean Brashear

Tycoon Dominic Santorini introduced himself to Lexie only as Nikos—but after an unplanned explosion of desire he couldn't help wondering if she was really a corporate spy. Could he trust the truth he felt in her every touch?

THE PREGNANT BRIDE Crystal Green

Kane's Crossing

Brooding tycoon Nick Cassidy married beautiful Meg Thornton when he learned she was carrying his enemy's baby. The perfect plan for revenge soon turned into love—but would Meg discover the truth?

0603/23a

FREE

4 BOOKS
AND A SURPRISE GIFT!

We would like to take this opportunity to thank you for reading this Silhouette® book by offering you the chance to take FOUR more specially selected titles from the Special Edition™ series absolutely FREE! We're also making this offer to introduce you to the benefits of the Reader Service™ —

★ FREE home delivery
★ FREE monthly Newsletter
★ FREE gifts and competitions
★ Exclusive Reader Service discount
★ Books available before they're in the shops

Accepting these FREE books and gift places you under no obligation to buy; you may cancel at any time, even after receiving your free shipment. Simply complete your details below and return the entire page to the address below. ***You don't even need a stamp!***

YES! Please send me 4 free Special Edition books and a surprise gift. I understand that unless you hear from me, I will receive 6 superb new titles every month for just £2.90 each, postage and packing free. I am under no obligation to purchase any books and may cancel my subscription at any time. The free books and gift will be mine to keep in any case.

E3ZED

Ms/Mrs/Miss/Mr ....Initials...................................
BLOCK CAPITALS PLEASE

Surname...

Address...

....

....Postcode ....

Send this whole page to:
UK: FREEPOST CN81, Croydon, CR9 3WZ
EIRE: PO Box 4546, Kilcock, County Kildare (stamp required)

Offer valid in UK and Eire only and not available to current Reader Service subscribers to this series. We reserve the right to refuse an application and applicants must be aged 18 years or over. Only one application per household. Terms and prices subject to change without notice. Offer expires 30th September 2003. As a result of this application, you may receive offers from Harlequin Mills & Boon and other carefully selected companies. If you would prefer not to share in this opportunity please write to The Data Manager at the address above.

Silhouette® is a registered trademark used under licence.
Special Edition™ is being used as a trademark.